FALLENDOR
The Sword of Sight

By Noah Cavalier

Every living thing has obstacles they must overcome.

To my mother, who is always supportive and helpful with a kind loving heart.

To my father, who watches down on me every day, I hope he can read this book one day.

To my four brothers and two sisters, who encourage me in their own different and unique ways but always with positivity.

To my dear sweet Natalie, family and friends who helped me along the way.

    Love ya, Noah

CHAPTER ONE

Adlar rushed down the dim hallway that led to his father's chambers. His heart pounded, drowning out the sound of his rapid footsteps. He halted at the door that separated him and the King. It relieved him when he was told to wait a little longer. Adlar hunched over and rested his palms on his knees. He raised his head as a loud crack of thunder echoed in the distance. Gazing out of a hall window, he noticed black clouds swarming in, casting a shadow over the city of Mouro, as rain lashed down darkening the city's walls.

    King Starian had ruled the great northern country of Raveria for thirty-four years. He had made peace with his enemies and used the country's wealth to support its arts. He kept to himself when he could, even if that meant journeying to the island of Rozann to get away from Mouro's chaos and busy streets. However, Starian's most recent excursion had been his last.

Five days ago, Starian returned from Rozann sick and weak. The king's visits to the island were executed in utmost secrecy. The people of Raveria, much like the rest of those in the world of Fallendor, were stubbornly independent and stayed within their borders. No one seemed to leave the city, let alone the country. His absence was unusual. However, King Starian admired travelling and learned much during his visits. The wisdom he'd gained on his two visits to Rozann was locked away in his mind forever, he did not have the time to share his secrets with his sons.

King Starian lay in his large canopy bed, his face as pale as a winter storm. The beauty of the room's ornate decorations contrasted starkly with the small, pale visage of a fine man in his final moments. Adlar was now joined by his two brothers outside the door of the bedroom. They nodded at the familiar sentries guarding their father's door and waited. It would be difficult for them to say goodbye. They had lost their mother after she gave birth to the twins. The young men lived without their mother for nineteen years, so they had devoted themselves to their loving father. King Starian called first for his eldest son.

Adlar, the tallest and broadest of the brothers clutched the lapels of his midnight-blue night robe, and crept into the room. He rubbed his hand over his face, from the top of his head, to his finely groomed beard.

"Adlar, my son. Come." Starian motioned to him.

"Father, please don't leave us," Adlar said quietly, almost begging.

"Son, you must be strong. Your brothers will need you. You are the heir of Raveria, and it is past time you took over this marvelous country as King. I have assigned your brothers important roles as stewards of Proda."

Adlar's eyes dampened. He wanted to say many things, but knew he had little time. "This is such an honor, Father."

"The people of Raveria will welcome your leadership. You will be a glorious King, Adlar."

"Thank you, Father."

Starian nodded slightly and continued, "Over the years, I have spent a great deal of time writing." He paused, indicating a row of leather-bound books on a nearby shelf. "My journals will be useful to you and your brothers. I hope the three of you will read them all one day."

Adlar stepped closer to hear his father's ailing voice, as his eyes watered.

"Only my head advisor and dear friend, Tymin knows of these books; not even your mother knew. They hold troves of memories and knowledge that will help any young king succeed," Starian said.

"Of course, Father. I will read them all."

"Good. Now get your brothers in here," Starian directed. The King was unsure if he had enough time to bid them farewell one-by-one. He was happy to have gotten a bit of time with his eldest, the heir to his throne.

Adlar pulled open the door and motioned his brothers inside. Though twins, they looked little alike. Agaras strolled through first, his long black hair falling in front of his face. Tobias, who was taller than Agaras, stood with his chin held high, his short brown hair perfect, not a strand out of place. The twin brothers joined their father and older brother.

King Starian looked at his boys and beamed a smile none would have expected from someone about to pass on.

"Tobias and Agaras, my sons, I have decided what I wish for you two to do," Starian said to his youngest sons.

They listened with gloomy eyes, both trying to hold back tears from creeping down their faces.

"I want you both to serve as joint stewards of Proda. That great city needs both of you to guide it. Your oldest cousin, Byrim awaits you both. He has been holding the position as steward there since my brother, Galion, passed. Byrim will be most happy to have you take over the stewardship."

"But Father, we want to stay here, in Mouro

with Adlar," Tobias protested.

"Your brother has his own commitments now. Adlar is King of Raveria so he must stay in the capital."

"I wanted to be king, Father," Agaras said abruptly.

"Adlar is the heir. When he has sons of his own his eldest will be the next heir of Raveria. I am sorry, Agaras. It is still a great honor to be steward. You and Tobias will do outstanding things together," Starian asserted.

Agaras scowled, distraught at the thought of not being king.

Adlar wasn't sure it would satisfy his brothers that he was chosen as heir. Though it was usually the case that the eldest son was the designated heir, it wasn't always what happened. Sometimes a younger son proved himself to be more capable than his oldest brother. Adlar had worked hard to make sure he was always worthy.

"I wish each of you could be a king," Starian continued calmly. "I know how much you all wanted it."

"And if the people don't like this?" Tobias asked.

"I have already made the process of making you boys stewards in Proda, so this won't come as a surprise to them. I am sure it will upset some, but I cannot save myself from dying. I am too weak..."

Starian's voice grew quieter with every crack

of his throat.

"Father, remember you said you would consider making me King of Raveria. You promised." Agaras's face grew red with impatience. He approached the head of his father's bed, bumping shoulders with Tobias.

Tobias was strong on his feet, but stumbled into Adlar. They stared at each other in astonishment, wide-eyed to see Agaras's reaction as their father lay dying.

"I did consider it, but I never promised to make you the King of Raveria, my boy," Starian said.

"I said you would be an excellent king. But Adlar is the heir and to make anyone else king would be unfair. You and Tobias will do a grand job in the west, Agaras." Starian choked on his words as he adjusted himself in bed.

Aldar reached to help him.

"You are a liar, Father! You are making an awful decision!" Agaras shouted and stormed toward the door.

"Agaras, you must stay," Starian said, coughing in distress.

Aldar placed his hand on the king's shoulder.

"Father, please. Rest."

Agaras turned to face his father. "I cannot. Something is telling me to leave."

He turned his back on his family and did not say another word. He left the king's chambers.

"Let him go then," Adlar said quietly.

"Boys, you need Agaras," King Starian muttered his last words. "Tobias, find him, try to reason with him and bring him back. Goodbye my sons."

Adlar stood and stepped close to Tobias, who was by the king's bedside. He placed his arms around Tobias, and they comforted each other. They watched their father breathe his last breath, devastated. With tearful eyes, the brothers left their beloved father and went their separate ways for the night.

Tobias and the new King Adlar, felt honored and humbled after learning what their father intended for them. Agaras was gone; it was no surprise that he got angry upon hearing their father's final instructions. Agaras was a jealous fool sometimes. However, it was only recently that he would sporadically become angry at his brothers or father for no real apparent reason.

This was something Agaras would just have to get over, they decided. They each handled grief differently, and perhaps Agaras just needed to be away.

Midnight drew near, and the rain, like the people of the always lively city, slowed down. The thunderstorm had drenched the entire capital, puddles and streams formed all throughout the courtyard. Tobias sulked out to the damp courtyard and sank down on an icy stone bench. His short brown hair dampened as water droplets fell from an overhanging branch. Tobias let out a deep sigh and couldn't help but think, losing my father will grieve me forever. He looked up to his father. His father had taken him out past the village and trained him with his bow and arrow. Tobias, a quick learner, mastered the skill. So, Starian trained him in the art of combat with a sword. No matter what Starian ever taught him, Tobias always wanted to learn more and continue spending time with his father. He would also go out late with his father and look up into the night sky to watch the stars. Raveria had some of the most beautiful starry nights, but perhaps it was because that time was spent with his father. Tobias gazed at the stars, he thought about what his father had said to him before passing, repeating the words to himself. He wondered why he would want to bring back his twin brother. He ran out on our father while he laid on his deathbed. Why bring that coward back? he thought. The idea of bringing his brother back drove him crazy because part of him wanted Agaras to remain gone forever. Tobias rolled over onto the cold bench which felt soothing on his back. He laid on the bench and stared into darkness, the rain finally stopped. He wandered in his thoughts all night; he did not go back inside to sleep. He contemplated what was the right thing to do. *Maybe it's too late*, he thought for a moment, maybe Agaras was too far away to find, or maybe Agaras didn't want to be found. Tobias didn't think Agaras had ever left the city of Mouro; he was worried about his twin. He did not know what trouble could stand in his way. No matter where Agaras went, his venture would be a lonely and perilous one.

It was a cool spring morning and Tobias was awakened in the courtyard by a soft mist, much more pleasant than the rain that had poured down the night before. Tobias felt he had to try to get Agaras back, as was his father's wish. He thought he could not be in charge of a city by himself, especially at the age of nineteen. He needed Agaras more than ever now. He got up from the cold courtyard bench, readied a horse from the stable and set out on his search. As he left the entrance to the city, the castle bells rang. Now that it was morning these bells could ring. This indicated to the rest of the people of Mouro that King Starian had died.

Adlar was in for a busy morning himself. He would have to address the people over their king's death. He was also to be crowned in front of the people in the capital within the coming days. Adlar was a caring and determined young man who wanted to follow in his father's steps and become a great king in Raveria, and he had the tools to be everything his father was.

Tobias still searched for his twin. He made his way through a small village called Rhen, just outside of Mouro. By the time he reached Rhen, the sun had started to shine through the branches of the trees that surrounded it. Birds whistling caught the ears of Tobias and made him smile. He always liked to hear them sing in the morning. He made his way past the village bakery. Fresh breads, herbs and cinnamon was something he found irresistible. He peeked inside to see the baker. She was a kind-looking woman but was a bit overweight likely due to all the taste testing over the years. Her face, so rosy and round that her cheeks forced her eyes closed whenever she smiled or spoke.

"Hello there boy," the baker said with a perky high-pitched voice. "I heard the bells from the city. Is everything okay?" she asked with cheeks as plump as a fresh-baked loaf.

"The king is dead. My father is gone." Tobias lowered his head.

"Oh no, I am so sorry. Come here," the baker kindly said with a hug.

"My brother stormed out and left, so I am out looking for him. Have you seen anyone wandering the village in haste?"

"I have seen no one suspicious all day."

"Alright. No worries. But I must go now, I have to be back in the capital by noon. The funeral is today, and everyone's invited."

"Here, take some for the road. I hope you find your brother," the baker said and handed Tobias a loaf of bread and two biscuits.

"Thank you so much." Tobias brought his palms together in appreciation, while he stepped back into the street.

Tobias continued through the village taking a bite of the fresh biscuit. It warmed his stomach. He loved having fresh bread and biscuits. His father used to take him to bakeries regularly, just the two of them. This was a perfect breakfast for Tobias who had not eaten since the previous day. He headed to a small lake at the end of the village, which was where he and his father used to go to watch the stars from time to time. Tobias always talked about this place, so it was no secret to the rest of the boys. He thought that might be where Agaras was. Tobias had no idea how Agaras would react if he found him. They got along well being twins, but they had their differences. The tall trees on the other side of the lake made a shadow on the water. The fog coming off the lake made it hard for Tobias to see much. He arrived at the shore, and saw a hooded figure. He approached the figure with caution. Tobias felt a chill from the gentle breeze that fluttered through the long grass. When he got closer the hooded figure turned around facing him.

"Tobias. What are you doing here?" Agaras asked as he removed his hood.

Tobias had a relieved look on his face at the sight of his brother Agaras. "Father told me to come find you," Tobias said.

"I did not think you or anyone else would come looking for me."
The two brothers hugged like they had been separated for years. But Agaras seemed on edge and lost.

"You should not have run off, Agaras. That was unwise of you."
Agaras shook his head.

"Father loved you," Tobias continued, but there was a brief silence. "Father was always there when we needed him. He made us a strong and loving family. He loved us Agaras, he was our king and our father, and you ran out on him while he was dying." His voice cracked.

"I don't know what happened. Something inside me just told me to leave immediately. It was a voice, or it was just my thoughts, I think. I can't go back now."

"Something? Like what?"

"You would not understand. I need to leave."

"Leave and go where?" Tobias' pupils doubled in size.

"It was my voice in my head, but when I left the city everything was normal again. Father never loved me!"

"Yes, he did."

"Father and you were always together, and I always got into trouble for no reason. I do not want to be a steward. I know I would be a better king than you or Adlar, but father was too blind to see it."

"Father is no foolish man, and I know if it was not for his love for all of us, he would have just made me king of Raveria, even over Adlar. He told me so himself, Agaras. Don't be unreasonable. This is our father you are speaking of."

"You are as crazy as he was to believe that," Agaras said firmly. "Father wants us in Proda, but I am greater than that, I want to rule all of Raveria, and of Fallendor. The rest of you are weak, I will rule all of Fallendor one day. Just wait and you will see." Tobias sniffed and rubbed his eyes, hoping for his brother not to see his tears. There was hurt and anger in Agaras's voice. No matter what Tobias said to reason with him, Agaras simply used it as a reason to leave.

"Let's return home. Father's funeral will be at noon. Come be with us during this time. Things will get better, I promise," Tobias said, giving one last hope his brother would oblige.

"And since we are now stewards," he continued, "we can discuss all the exciting things we will do. Doesn't that excite you Agaras? Proda is such an exciting city for us to govern. Think of all the fun we would have. We will miss you if you don't come back."

Agaras looked skyward, then down to the ground. He started breathing heavily and knew how much his brother wanted him to come back alongside him. Agaras quickly thought that Raveria wasn't the place for him anymore. He did not know where this feeling was coming from; it was new to him. Agaras put his hood back on and turned his back to Tobias.

"I am not coming back with you; I don't belong here. I can't live under the shadows of my brothers any longer. Even Father must have seen this. I am going to see our uncle in Tatilan."

"Why Tatilan? You don't even know how to get there."

"I know it is south of here. I'll just make my way south. I don't care if I die along the way. It will be better than staying in Raveria."

"You can't go!" Tobias interrupted. "Have you not heard about what happens in Tatilan? Where is this coming from, Agaras?"

"I heard it's a wonderful place. Father told us otherwise to scare us from asking him questions I imagine." Agaras slowly made his way away from the shore and up a hill.

Tobias knew this was goodbye and there was no stopping Agaras. His heart was set on leaving. Tobias stayed by the lake in doubt as he watched his brother storm away into the morning haze. Agaras got to the top of the hill and turned to Tobias.

"It was me," Agaras said "I killed Father!"

Tobias stood still and lowered his gaze. Tobias tried to process the devastating news he had just learned. He did not want to believe what Agaras had just said. It couldn't possibly be true. When Tobias looked up, Agaras was already out of sight due to the thick fog that came off the lake, so he could not even learn if this was some sort of ploy. He thought it was impossible that Agaras killed their loving father.

Tobias searched around him for answers, as if he would see an omen in the fog. He had too many questions that needed to be answered. There was no time to run after him—there was the funeral.

He also had to go back and pack his belongings, as he was to leave for his new home later in the day. Tobias gathered himself up and dragged his feet away from the damp shore of the lake, making his way back to Mouro with tears of disbelief in his eyes and a look of utter confusion. He was unsure how he would tell Adlar what Agaras had just told him.

Agaras returned to the makeshift tent he had made next to a large tree across the lake. He would often go out there to camp by himself. When Agaras left Mouro, he gathered a few supplies. Anyone who saw him leaving the city would not have been suspicious because of how frequently he left. He found peace being alone under the night sky. Agaras sat by the small fire that he made. He caught himself staring into the yellow flame and contemplated if he should go back to Mouro. Even if just to say goodbye to his father. Tobias had told him that the funeral was due to happen later that day, so he had some time to think and still make it back if he wished. Although Agaras kept to himself growing up, he was a wise young man. He felt like his other brothers were favored over him, which was why he took to camping alone outside the city and in the wilderness. Agaras recalled a night he was out alone and heard some voices behind a shrub. He looked through the bushes and saw his father, Starian and Tymin talking. Agaras remembered vividly what they said that night. Starian had asked Tymin what they should do with his crown. Agaras was curious and later heard them say that no one in Fallendor must know about the power of the crown. Agaras's curiosity urged him to keep coming back to this same spot. He found out that this was where Tymin and Starian would discuss anything related to the crown. Agaras spent many night's listening to his father's conversations with Tymin. He knew the secrets, but he never told a soul. He coveted the crown more than ever when he learned of its power.

Thinking back on this gave Agaras a sudden thought. He pulled out a key he had tied around his neck. It started out as a little game to see if he would get caught. But over time, he enjoyed spying on his father so much it became a habit. Perhaps the king would say something good about Agaras.

He was reminded of a day that he followed his father to a door at the back of the capital. The door was unknown to many. Its location made it very uncommon for anyone to use it, so it was overlooked. It was near the King's Hall which only the king and members of his family could come near. King Starian and his closest advisors were the only ones who used the door. Agaras also wanted to use the door secretly, but could never get the key without his father realizing. He saw his father constantly use the door time and time again. Starian used this door to avoid shuffling through the busy streets and crowds of the capital. Agaras knew his father kept the key around his neck. Agaras realized the key was on his father's bedside table when he was in his chambers with his two brothers. So, he took the key without the others noticing and kept it for himself. Agaras tightly held the key in his hand and thought about how many times he witnessed his father use the key to come and go into the city. He decided he was going to use the key once more to sneak into Mouro. Not to see his father, but to steal the crown and bring it to his uncle in Tatilan. Even though Agaras had never met his uncle, he heard stories that he was not the kindest king in Fallendor. Agaras thought that if he could bring the crown of Raveria to the south and tell him of its power then he would get the respect he had craved. Agaras wondered if it would be best to wait until it was dark before attempting to break in…but he knew the city better than anyone and was aware that it would be quieter in the kingdom when daylight disappeared.

      Night fall was still a long time away, and the window of time for him to get back to the city was narrowing. It would become very difficult to steal the crown once Adlar's crowning occurred. Agaras was not certain when this would be, but he knew he had to act fast.

CHAPTER TWO

The bells in the Kingdom of Mouro were rang once more. It was noon, and the king's people had gathered inside the courtyard for the funeral. Everyone had come together to express their condolences to their former king's family. Tobias was already back in the capital and was quick to find his brother, Adlar. He joined his brother on the stage in front of the crowd, but still wondered to himself how he could tell Adlar about what Agaras had said.

The internal battle haunted him. Was Agaras kidding? Was it just a way to distract him and run off?

The two brothers mourned, much like the rest of the kingdom. The packed crowd watched in silence as their beloved King Starian was carried through the streets and taken to the burial grounds outside the city. All that could be heard were birds tweeting and the people of Mouro sniffling and crying as they watched their king's body leave the city.

Starian's sons looked devastated. Tobias looked as if he hadn't slept in weeks. His blue pants were ragged and his crumpled dirty shirt looked as if he had run through a forest of thorns forty times. Tobias never was one to care much about what he wore. He mainly wore hand-me-downs from his older brother that he and Agaras would fight over. Tymin, their father's closest advisor, accompanied the two brothers. He was a tall slender man with a thick brown beard. He looked as if he had been crying for weeks. His eyes were red and his eyelashes were frayed and wet. Tymin gave the brothers a subtle nod and rubbed his eyes. He was to address the people of Mouro as he stood upon a stage overlooking the crowds.

"People of Mouro, it is a time of mourning as we say goodbye to our dear king," Tymin said as his deep voice crackled.

"However, this is also a time for celebration as we welcome our new king, King Adlar."

"All hail King Adlar!" shouted the crowd instantly, as Adlar returned the cheer with a humbling wave from where he stood.

"Adlar is a brave man who shows great leadership and cares for everybody he knows. These qualities will make him a great king and leader to you all for many years to come. Please welcome your new king now as he addresses you all for the first time." Adlar strode forth immediately to address the crowd.

"People of Raveria, it is my privilege to serve you as king. I have lived in this beautiful kingdom my whole life. I will lead like my father for you. All of Raveria will be in great hands," King Adlar said confidently with a deep clear voice. "I will maintain peace and prosperity in this great country of Raveria for as long as I am your king."

The confidence in Adlar's voice made him sound ready to be a great king. A sad day had turned joyous for some, although King Adlar still felt hollow inside. He fought back tears of sadness, as the people of Mouro chanted his name once more.

"All hail King Adlar!" the crowds erupted.

Hearing the crowds roar his name jolted Adlar with the reality that he was now King of Raveria, and his father was gone forever. He looked back at Tobias; whose sad face reflected the same pain. Tymin soon dispersed the crowds and turned to the new king and his brother.

"My king. Your father would be proud to see this day," Tymin said with a faint bow.

"He would indeed. We are all in this together," Adlar replied with a smile. He continued.

"The two of us will maintain Raveria's unity as one."

"Certainly. Come boys, let us walk."

Tymin led Tobias and Adlar through an alleyway by the courtyard, which met up with a set of stairs that led to the top of the city walls. The steps to the wall were damp from the last few days of rain. They could hear a splash with every step they took.

"I fear darkness could be upon us," Tymin said as they reached the top of the city walls. "Your father should not have died. He was only in his fifties."

"Why do you think that, Tymin?" Adlar asked.

"I just have a feeling Starian had more life to give, he had no reason to get sick. I could be wrong. The world is a funny place sometimes," Tymin mused. He had hardly said this when a sudden wind came barreling in along with gray clouds. "Ah, great," Tymin said. "The clouds are flooding in. Looks like it might rain again."

"I have always hated the second month of spring," Tobias said rolling his eyes. "Way too much rain," He whined, "But summer is upon us thankfully."

"I have important things to talk to you boys about, let's make our way inside," Tymin said.

The three wandered along the city walls and

headed toward the king's chambers. They headed down steps leading from the western tower. They passed the King's Hall, which was where members of the council would discuss matters alongside the king, as they ate their meals. The King's Hall was built from rust-colored granite stone. Large pillars graced the entranceway of its large stone door, which was engraved with flowers and the faces of the past kings of Raveria in astonishing detail. Adlar and Tobias could not help but stare at the detail in passing. They never noticed such beauty before, even though they had passed the same doors many times growing up.

"Come, we are not going inside the hall today," Tymin said as he turned to see the brothers mesmerized by the door.

The king's chamber was also where the rest of his advisors and members of the council stayed. It was so large you could see the top from miles outside the city walls. The king's room was on the ninth floor, which also had a gorgeous view of the city and its surroundings. Tymin continued to lead the boys past a small pond at the front of the entrance to the castle. The pond was crystal clear blue with tiny orange fish swimming around frantically. Tobias reached inside the pond to splash away the fish. Much to the refreshing delight Tobias had, they continued their walk up the dark stone steps to the top. When they finally arrived at the king's room Tymin demanded Tobias close the door tightly behind them, as if he were not tired enough from these stairs.

"You both know this was where your father stayed. It was his, but it is yours now, Adlar," Tymin explained.

"I never spent much time here to be honest, Father was always protective of his room," Adlar said.

"Do either of you know that I went with your father to Rozann twenty-three years ago?" Tymin asked.

"Like we said, our Father never really told us much," Tobias replied, who had sat down on a wooden stool.

"You may not know this, but the crown of Raveria is very powerful," Tymin whispered.

"Your father wanted you to read about it in his own words. So Adlar, read the books he left you. I can tell you more about it all after you read them. If you have any questions."

"We never knew Father went to this island, except for when he got back almost a week ago," Adlar stated.

"It would not seem right to your father if I had told you. So please, just read the books," Tymin said.

"Also, I should mention that you won't need a large gathering to finish your crowning. Just a small group of members from the council will be there."

"Tymin, I understand why Father wanted to make me king. These people have already shown me so much love and compassion. I had not even had my crown on yet and the people still cheered for me,"

Adlar stood confidently. "I am glad they have shown faith in me and accept me as their new king. I have been through enough for one day, though. So, I am glad we are doing my crowning another day."

"Yes, of course," Tymin said. "Your father was a smart man."

"You will both make brilliant leaders here in Raveria. I will arrange with the council soon to discuss plans for your crowning in the coming days. That will give all of us time to rest."

"In the meantime, Adlar, I seriously suggest you read your father's books. You will find them very useful as king," Tymin said, pointing to a large wooden shelf with books piled on top of each other.

"What should I do?" Tobias asked calmly.

"I am sure your cousin Byrim won't mind you waiting a few days before arriving in Proda," Tymin explained. "Stay a few more days to see your brother Adlar's crowning."

"I am tired, you two. I must first take a nap," Adlar muttered with tired eyes.

"Very well. We will leave you to it," Tymin said, as they left Adlar's room.

"Tobias, I will leave you for a while as well. I have to make sure I arrange everything with the other members of the council for the crowning," Tymin explained.

"That is okay. I will be fine wandering the streets of the city. Then I will likely have some of Mouro's finest wine. Join me later for a glass if you wish," Tobias replied.

"Certainly, I will come find you at the pub later. We can discuss some things you may want to know about your new city Proda."

"Great, see you soon, Tymin."

Tobias had always been a casual drinker, even at a young age. He never liked the taste of wines and ales, but developed a joy for drinking with friends, especially recently. He thought this would be a perfect way to pass the time while he was alone, and he made his way to one of the busier pubs in the kingdom. Any night it was packed with interesting folk, from all walks of life. Some came in groups; others drank to their loneliness.

Tobias noticed the only free chair in the pub. It was a chaotic place, it seemed to him that everyone was trying to be heard from one side of the bar to the next. Tobias's eyes lit up when he sat at a corner table.

The man across from him gave him an uneasy glare. "Curious place for a young boy like yourself to be is it not?"

"Seems to me it is the place to be on a rainy night," Tobias said, ordering the bartender over for a drink with the wave of his hand.

"Suit yourself, I spend all my time here and I've never seen you," the man said with a smile.

Tobias thought he'd never see this man smile in such a way based on the initial glare he was given.

"Just here waiting for someone. Going to calm the nerve with a drink or two, my father was the king you know."

"Why did you not say so, boy? Hey lady, bring us your finest ale," the man said, who was suddenly warming up to Tobias, now that he knew he was the late king's son.

"Have a drink, I got you covered all night. I will keep you company until your friend gets here."

"Thank you, sir, what is your name anyways?"

"Dann. Blame my mother for the dumb name, must be why I drink so much."

"My name is Tobias. I like the name Dann. It's not too bad." Tobias forgot for a moment he was waiting for Tymin—he wasn't sure how much time had passed.

Dann suddenly stood, sliding his drink toward Tobias and stumbled his way through a wall of people without saying another word. Tobias was alone at the table and had nothing left to do but drink.

A few hours must have passed and Adlar was woken up from his nap by a faint knock on the door. He rubbed his eyes and rose to open the door.

"Adlar. I hope I did not disturb you," Tymin said.

"Is it late?" Adlar asked with a subtle yawn.

"It is just after supper," Tymin replied. "I am just here for the crown. We are not ready for the coronation yet but I just wanted to bring the crown to the King's Hall now so we can be set up for it."

"I never even noticed the crown sitting over there until now, let me go grab it for you."

"No rush, my king."

"Thank you for doing all this by the way, it really means a lot," Adlar said, handing the crown to Tymin.

"It is my job after all," Tymin said with a smile.

"Have you seen Tobias?" Adlar asked.

"He said earlier that he was going for a walk. I was supposed to meet him for a drink later. I am sure he is well."

The night was still young, but the city was already quiet. When daylight disappeared the people of Mouro retreated to their homes or to pubs. Tymin was making his way back to the King's Hall; a decent ten-minute walk from Adlar's room.

Tymin heard something coming from a dark alley to his right just before he reached the entranceway of the hall. The carvings on the door were merely shadows that shimmered in the light from a couple of torches. Tymin turned away toward the direction of the sound that had disappeared.

"Who is there?" Tymin asked.
The night was filled with a soft hum of the kingdom falling asleep.

"Hello! Is anybody there? You know you should not be loitering in this place," Tymin said as he approached the dark alley, still unable to see or hear anyone.

"Hello old man," Agaras said as he crept out of the shadows.

Tymin could only see the whites of Agaras's eyes before it was too late. Agaras had a large knife in his hand and quickly plunged it into Tymin's stomach. Agaras swiftly put his hands over Tymin's face to prevent any screams of pain. Blood poured out of Tymin as Agaras quickly dragged him into the alleyway so he would be out of sight from anyone passing by. The crown had dropped from Tymin's hand as he became motionless. Agaras quickly dropped Tymin's dead body further into the alley and ran back to grab the crown. A shadow hid the smear of blood that followed Agaras. The darkness would only hide the traces to Tymin until morning. Agaras held onto the crown tightly and fled out of the city.

Agaras, having escaped through the back door of the city, ran toward a local stable. He stole a horse—but was it really stealing? —and was on his way to Tatilan. He knew it would be a very long journey and had no idea how to get there. He just hoped he could find help along the way as he headed south. Agaras knew he had to leave Raveria for good now. It was never his plan to kill an innocent man, especially a member of the council and dear friend of the family. It wouldn't be long until someone found Tymin's dead body back in the city. Agaras wondered if his brothers would be more disappointed about him killing Tymin or stealing the crown of Raveria. He just knew he had to leave quickly.

CHAPTER THREE

The sun rose, and a new day came. The people in Mouro made their way to the markets. It was a regular routine here. Tobias didn't differ. He woke up in a small ripped-up bed with no blankets and no pillow. His head pounded from a night of drinking. However, he had an enjoyable night at a local pub, drinking all the best wines and ales the capital had to offer. Tobias sat up in bed, but which was more odd: the ragged bed he ended up in at the pub, or the fact that Tymin didn't show up for a drink last night as he said he would? Tobias made his way back to Adlar's room and knocked loudly on Adlar's door, who was quick to open it.

    "You're up, brother," Tobias said.

    "Yes, of course I am up. No thanks to you,"

Adlar mumbled as he yawned.

"Where is Tymin? I told him to come for a drink with me last night, but he never showed," Tobias asked.

"He was probably busy getting my coronation ready. He came to get my crown to set things up."

"Let's go to the King's Hall then. See if Tymin wants us to do anything else before your crowning."

"Let me get dressed," Adlar said and turned to grab a plain white shirt draped over a chair. "Or now that I am King, does that mean I can demand you dress me?"

Tobias tossed his head back. "Yeah right, brother."

Tobias and Adlar strolled down the steps from the chambers and headed toward the King's Hall. They noticed a gathering of people once they got closer.

"What is going on here?" Adlar asked.

"My king, Tymin is dead. We found him this morning in the alley," a guard said.

Tobias and Adlar rushed through the crowd to see for themselves. Adlar and Tobias's mouths dropped at the sight of the head advisor. Tymin's face was the color of light lavender and had white blotches under his eyes. The trail of blood from his stomach painted the streets a murky bronze.

"Who did this?" Adlar asked.

"Nobody knows. He was just found like this,"

another guard said.

"Where is the crown? He had it last night," Adlar said frantically.

A woman's voice rose over the crowd. "I think I know who did this."

"Maria?" Tobias asked.

"What are you doing here, Maria?" Adlar questioned.

"I heard a commotion while I was on my walk and came to see. I know your brother better than anyone. He wanted to be king so bad. I wouldn't be surprised if he did this," Maria said, revealing her pale face.

"Agaras has been gone for two days though," Tobias replied.

"Did you see him?" Adlar asked, obviously desperate for answers.

"Like I said. I am only guessing he did this. But I didn't see a thing," Maria said softly. "I know his recent outbursts surprised us all."

"Arrest this woman until we know for certain," Adlar demanded as he approached her.

"No, Aldar. We should wait until we know for certain," Tobias said, holding his older brother back.

"Tobias, she knows something about our brother she isn't telling us," Adlar suggested.

"Perhaps, but if the people of this city see us arrest someone, questions will be asked. We can't let them know there may be a murderer amongst us. It will only frighten everyone," Tobias explained.

"Very well, Maria, leave here at once. We always suspected you and Agaras would stay together, despite what you both told everyone," Adlar sent her away with the wave of his hand.

Maria and Agaras had a love history, though the bags under her eyes would suggest otherwise. They were lovers, but a feud between Starian and Maria's father had forced them apart. Maria's father was one of Mouro's blacksmiths and he wanted more money for work he had done. He was a greedy man but also needed more money to help feed his family. He felt King Starian had the wealth to give him more but Starian believed all blacksmiths should be paid the same wage. When Starian declined his offer, Maria's father said she had to leave Agaras and never see him again. Maria and Agaras stayed together and kept it hidden from everyone else.

Could the rumors be true? Could Maria and Agaras have been seeing each other in secret? Adlar's scrunched face suggested he might have wondered the same thing.

Adlar and Tobias turned around from the small crowd of people and whispered between themselves.

"If Maria thinks Agaras did this, then it makes him a wanted man. Anyone that murders a member of my council will be punished by death," Adlar said.

"Even my brother."

"If he has the crown, he will take it to our uncle in Tatilan," Tobias said.

"Tobias, we have to find Agaras and question him. We need to get to Tatilan before he does if that's where he's heading."

"We do. I think we should tell Theo to come with us. He should know about his father. I will head out right now to bring him here. Then we can decide what we will do together."

"Agaras could be still in the castle. Tell any guards you see to search for him at once."

"Of course, brother."

"Tobias, ride north and get Theo. Tell him the King of Raveria requests him. Ride quickly."

"Farewell Adlar. I hope to arrive back soon," Tobias said as he made his way to the city stable to leave on his journey north.

Adlar turned back to the bystanders that stood upon the dead body of Tymin. "Someone, clean this mess up. We can't let blood rotten our streets."

Adlar was saddened to see Tymin gone. He'd have to find a new lead advisor to take his place. Since he was no longer having his crowning, he could use his time reading. King Adlar could spend all day reading his father's writings, and that's exactly what he intended to do. He made his way back to his room and went straight to the shelf of books, where he grabbed the first book he saw and started to read.

12th day of the 7th month of summer of the 1180th year

I had a lovely night with my Queen. We do enjoy walking outside the city looking at all of the nature Raveria has to offer. I had the thought while walking with her that I should begin journaling and writing my experiences as king. So, one day when I have children, they can use this as a tool to help them. This will be my first entry and I hope to continue writing weekly, if not daily entries. Myself and my dear sweet wife talked about what our future holds. We both want to have sons, but it is also our wish to have a little girl as well. What a beautiful and peaceful world we live in, to raise a family in. Starian.

Adlar turned another page of the large dusty book.

23rd day of the 8th month of summer of the 1180th year

When I was a young boy, my father, Villard changed the ways of Raveria for the first time in almost a century. There was a great rebellion and conflicts were rampant among the people of Raveria. Everyone was fighting for power, even those with no claim to the throne. King Villard decided he would assign stewards to help him take charge of the cities. With such a massive country, it was difficult to control the land all by himself, especially with the people fighting amongst themselves. Order was instantly restored, and things stayed that way for several years. Before this change, each of Raveria's cities was governed by its own king, but over time, this system brought more chaos and corruption. I have thought long and hard about going back to those old ways of having a king in each city rather than stewards, to benefit my future sons one day. There have not been three kings in Raveria, since well before I was even born. Fallendor is a world that has finally found peace again. I have currently decided against going back to Raveria's old ways; I have fought hard to maintain peace in all of Fallendor and improved the culture of Raveria. I do hope the sons I have can still work together in harmony and stay strong as a nation, despite only one becoming king. I hope all of Raveria's future king's will keep this tradition strong and maintain its peace forever. Starian.

Adlar examined his new room and was overwhelmed by the number of books. Adlar realized some of these books were written well before he was born. Clearly his father continued with his journal entries. Would he have time to read them all? He let out a sigh and dropped the book, letting it hit the ground. Adlar wrote a quick letter at his table, called for his maiden and handed it to her. A message to inform the others in Raveria that Agaras was a wanted man.

Adlar felt lost, but he had to wait for Theo and Tobias to return back to the capital. Adlar sauntered out to his balcony off the ninth floor and heard the tweeting of a small brown finch. The little bird made a pleasant sound. Its beautiful song was enough to perk Adlar up and made him smile. The late morning skies were beaming with joy. As Adlar approached closer to the edge of the balcony the finch fluttered off. Adlar wondered to himself what it would be like to be able to fly like that little bird. Being able to fly anywhere in this world would be an amazing gift he thought. He continued to stare off into the luscious green forests and bright blue skies of Raveria. The thought of being able to fly would certainly make it easier to find Agaras he thought. Of course, for a human to fly was impossible, but Adlar enjoyed having these imaginative thoughts.

    Adlar continued scanning off the edge of his balcony. Down the road, a wagon approached the city. He recognized the local villager who was delivering the daily supplies for the markets. Adlar knew this villager was coming from the harbor by the wagon packed full of fish. A fish even fell off the bumpy wagon and on to the dirt road. Adlar had an idea when he thought of the harbor. Small fishing boats might be useful to get to Tatilan. The waters of the Grey Sea were said to be treacherous, and Fallendor was yet to build ships durable enough to sail the rough waters. The small fishing boats kept to the bay and close to the coast to fish. If he could only get large ships built, one's big enough and strong enough to sail the sea. Any ship of such size would take a long time to build. He continued to watch the wagon from his balcony and thought of his friend, Maxall. Maxall was someone who could build, and he was a fine craftsman as well. Perhaps Maxall would make a good new head advisor. He should pay his old friend Maxall a visit.

Adlar left his chambers in a hurry without even putting on any suitable clothing other than a sleeping gown. He made his way to Maxall's shop which was past the markets. He was always in his shop carving new projects. He was a great builder of all things including small fishing boats, so Adlar hoped he could attempt to build the first ship Raveria had ever seen before, but time wouldn't be on his side.

Adlar paced through the busy markets and arrived at Maxall's shop. Maxall slaved away as usual. He had a thick black beard, and very curly hair that Maxall smacked out of his eyes consistently. It was apparent that he had been working for hours by the amount of wood chips tangled in his hair. Adlar wondered why Maxall hadn't shaved it all off by now. He had been crafting a small wooden figure, one that looked as if it may have been for a child. Maxall saw Adlar at his doorstep, so he dusted off his hands.

"Adlar, my friend. My king. So good to see you," Maxall said with a smile, and lowered his head.

"My dear friend, I have questions for you," Adlar replied.

"Ask away, my lord."

"First, I know we don't see each other like we used to when we were younger."

"I just thought it would be great to have someone like you join my council and be my advisor," Adlar suggested. "You can still maintain work here. I would only need you to appear occasionally for any future councils."

"I would be honored," Maxall joyfully said. "I miss seeing you as much as we used to. You do know where to find me, however."

"You are right, Maxall. Now that you're a member of my council I have another request," Adlar inquired.

"I know you'll answer all of my questions when they arise," Maxall explained. "If I have any, but being an advisor would be an honor, and I accept this challenge. What is your other request, my king?"

"Can you build me a ship? One big enough to sail across the Grey Sea?" Adlar asked.

"Oof, that is some request," Maxall said. "But you've come to the right place. The late king asked myself, my brother, and my father many years ago to build a ship," Maxall continued. "No one in all of Fallendor had ever made a ship of such size."

"So, what happened?"

"We were close to finishing but my mother got sick. As you know," Maxall said. "My father had to help with her so we couldn't complete it. Haven't worked on it since."

"Can you finish it now? How long would it take?" Adlar asked.

"I would say a week, maybe two before it could be ready to sail," Maxall guessed.

"Maxall, this is exciting. You are Raveria's finest woodsmen for a reason, your brother is quite the craftsman as well. Get him and some men to join you. Gather any wood you need to complete this ship."

"It is important that we get to Tatilan before Agaras so we can stop him, and we need a big ship so we can take soldiers in case of an attack. Make sure there is a lower deck with bed's and storage space too. It will be a few days journey I am sure," Adlar continued.

"There is already a lower deck. Your father had grand ideas to sail the Grey Sea," Maxall admitted.

"Maxall, I know you can do this. In time I will ask you to build many ships. But for now, one will do. I would like the ship ready to set sail by the next full moon." Adlar said.

Maxall smiled at Adlar, knowing his stubborn friend would be persistent and would not stop until he got his wish.

"I will do this for you, not because you are my king, but because you are my friend. I don't think I have to remind you, but the next full moon is over a week away…"

"Well, I suggest you get working. Gather all

the men you can find. More hands make for lighter work."

Maxall grabbed a few supplies and headed out of his shop. "Is that all you wanted, my friend? I should go to the harbor to finish the ship," he said, and stepped through his doorway.

"Ah, yeah, for now. But I do need a queen Maxall, this city is filled with interesting people, I could never find anyone to marry here."

"Adlar, you are quite the jokester, I am no expert when it comes to love. I haven't gazed into the eyes of a woman in a long time."

"However, does your father not have loads of books in your room? Read them, he may even have tips about how to fall in love in one of them," Maxall said jokingly.

Adlar shared a smile with Maxall and hugged.

"Farewell my friend, I look forward to seeing your progress soon, take care." He walked back through the markets.

Adlar made his way through the city once more and back to his room. He thought it was the perfect time to continue reading his father's books.

When Adlar got to his room, he walked back over to his pile of books and picked up a different one. These books were covered in dust, as if untouched. Adlar gave a light blow to the book he picked up and a large dust cloud filled the room. Adlar sat down on the edge of his bed, opened a different book from the shelf and read.

17th day of the 1st Month of Winter of the 1193rd Year

I have just arrived from the council of Kings. We discussed how we can continue to remain in peace in this great world of Fallendor. Everyone voted me Ruler of Fallendor. All but my brother Larrius who was jealous with the decision. At first, I accepted this with great honor. But I slowly realized that it would be best for Fallendor to remain the way it was with having a King in each nation. So, I gave up the title of Ruler of Fallendor. Larrius has been in Tatilan for years, ever since our father said he would never be King of Raveria. The King's council who voted me Ruler of Fallendor just added to Larrius's hate for me. He's quite the jealous boy. Larrius is much younger than me after all, so he should be okay. He's had a happy life in Tatilan and the south is much more suited for him. At the council he suggested we alternate being ruler of Fallendor. Every ten years a new ruler alternate from Azden, Tatilan or Raveria. Larrius thought this would be the fairest thing to do, but everyone disagreed. We are all kings in our own countries, peaceful and happy which is how we agreed to keep it. Larrius is king in the south. The current king of Azden, Beleg, will be passing his crown over to his son soon. Azden has always been a nation stuck in the middle of our family. But it was how Fallendor was divided at the beginning of time. Azden always had kings of the same blood, so their line has never been broken. Then there is me, King of Raveria. It's simpler this way. My brother Larrius is just jealous of the title of being ruler that I temporarily had. He'll be okay with it. Certainly not a reason to get angry. My queen awaits me for supper, we're having my favorite, beef stew with spiced carrots. Starian

After reading, Adlar realized that his father was once Ruler of Fallendor. Although it was brief, this seemed interesting to Adlar because the title "Ruler of Fallendor" did not exist anymore. King Adlar grazed quickly through the next few pages of his father's book. He saw the next page and had information on when his father and Tymin went to Rozann.

It was still light out. He was hoping he would still have time to read all about his father's trip to Rozann. Instead, Adlar requested his captain to assemble some men and crew to join him in the knight's room. They were to discuss strategy and their plan for the voyage south to Tatilan. King Adlar wanted his men in peak condition, so he ordered his men to train until the ship was ready to sail. The king was uncertain of the size of this ship but was hoping to have at the very least thirty men aboard.

Adlar spent all evening with General Cirdan and their soldiers going through strategy and training.

"My king, shall we continue training? The rain is now pouring down. And the night is late." Cirdan was a broad man and tall in stature. He served the kingdom as general already for many years so was highly respected in Mouro.

"There was a glimmer of moonlight but you are right Cirdan, retreat your men indoors and we'll continue tomorrow and the day after," Adlar said, rubbing his eyes and giving off a loud yawn.

"See you tomorrow at first light, King Adlar."

The moonlight cut through the sideways rain as Adlar himself returned to find shelter. Seeing the determination in these fighters' eyes, King Adlar thought it would be a successful mission south. He felt informing his men of his plan was more important than reading.

He finished up the night training his men after long hours. He was too tired to read any more of the books for another day anyways. Ironically it was reading that generally put Adlar to sleep, so maybe he could have done such a thing. King Adlar knew preparing his troops until his brother Tobias and Theo arrived in the capital, was wisest, besides it was late and sleep was much needed for the exhausted king. He hoped it wouldn't take much longer, but days of training could do everyone good.

CHAPTER FOUR

After another day and a bit of intensive training and hard work, King Adlar's troops were well prepared, trained, and ready for their journey to Tatilan. Adlar knew the deadline he had given Maxall was approaching and he decided to go to see Maxall's progress in Adon Harbor. Adlar made his way out through the courtyard toward the stables. On horseback it would be a quick trek to the harbor.

The king arrived before noon. He searched the hectic streets. The harbor was always a busy place, no matter the time, with scores of vendors and shops. The scent of fresh fish and delicate pastries made Adlar's stomach roar. When he locked eyes with a woman selling fish, and when she smiled at him, and she was so indescribably beautiful that Adlar didn't know if it was his heart or his stomach telling him just how hungry he was. As he stood in the line of customers for a small bite to eat, Adlar admired her rose-pink skin and thought she was the most gorgeous woman he had ever seen. Her sandy brown hair was tied up and her brown eyes sparkled as if they were responsible for lighting the night sky.

"Hello, sir," the woman said.

"Uh, hello," Adlar replied nervously.

"Can I help you with something?" she asked, and it was plain that she didn't know who Adlar really was.

"Actually, I am okay now. I found who I am looking for," Adlar replied, and stepped out of line.

He must not have been too hungry after all, rather, more thrilled about seeing Maxall waving him over behind a crowd, than the fish he had still not ordered.

"My king, come and see!" Maxall shouted. Adlar quickly followed him out of the crowds and toward the shoreline.

"Look, isn't it spectacular?" Maxall pointed toward a tall ship.

"It's complete. It was easier for us to finish than we thought. My people are obtaining more wood as we speak, so we will get the rest of your ships done when we can."

"Maxall, this is wonderful, and three days ahead of schedule as well," Adlar replied.

The king was excited to set sail. He hoped his

brother Tobias and Theo would be in the capital to join him soon. He wanted to leave for Tatilan before the following sunset. It was not certain that they would make it to Tatilan by sea before Agaras, who though was on foot, as he did have almost a two week head start. It was estimated by Maxall that the journey would take a few days to get south by ship, but no one knew for certain. Adlar hoped this mighty ship could get them south fast enough.

Adlar paced to the fence his horse was hosted, when he bumped into the woman from the fish monger's again.

"I apologize, your highness," she said with a bow.
Adlar could only stare in awe at the woman, amazed by her beauty.

"A woman as beautiful as yourself does not need to bow to me, my lady. I am rushing to get back to the castle and didn't watch my step," he replied.
She blushed. "I am Livia. It is a pleasure to have run into you my king. I had no idea earlier that you were the new King of Raveria," she admitted, and seemed completely embarrassed.

"I don't come to this village much, but I was here because I was seeing if my crew and I could leave on a ship tomorrow," King Adlar replied.

"How exciting it must be to be the king, and travel in a large ship," Livia said softly, "and also get to wander the city and live in castles, I've never even been to the capital before."

Adlar hopped back on his horse and stretched out his hand.

"Come, my lady. Let me take you to the capital then. I will show you what the city of Mouro is all about."

"I hope we are not too long; my father will wonder where I went, but I will come with you. I am excited to see all the splendors of the capital," Livia said with a smile.

Adlar returned the smile and helped Livia mount his horse behind him, Livia gripped Adlar's waist tightly. Adlar smiled from ear to ear. The two left the harbor and started the twenty-minute ride back to Mouro.

When they arrived, Livia was instantly amazed at the beauty and sheer size of the city. The stunning backdrop of forests made beige walls of the city pop out like the sun on a clear summer day. King Adlar's nine-story castle could be seen from far away towering above all.

"Come on, let's head inside," Adlar said.

"This place is fascinating," Livia gushed.

"How have I never been here?"

"I think so too. The view from my balcony is quite stunning." Adlar grinned.

"I want to see it all, especially the view. I never see anything other than fish and villagers."

"Follow me then," Adlar said with a dashing smile.

Livia followed Adlar closely as he walked up

a staircase that led to the top of the walls. One could survey the entire city from there while avoiding the chaos of the markets which had started to close up for the day. Past the city walls one could see for miles, if it weren't for the forests blocking parts of the view. Adlar pointed toward different places in the city: pubs, blacksmiths, courtyards, interesting people to note. Adlar took Livia's hand and helped her down the steps of the wall into the king's sector. They walked through the gardens and arrived at the castle and walked up the steps to the ninth-floor balcony. Livia ran ahead to the edge to get a better look.

"Wow, Adlar. This view is beautiful, you can really see everything from here," Livia exclaimed, astonished.

"I come here almost every day. Looking out from such heights is so relaxing," Adlar explained.

"You are lucky. I think I should head back to the harbor though. My father does not like it when he does not know where I am."

"Why do you have to hurry? It is getting late, are you sure you want to leave when it is this dark?"

"My king, thank you for taking the time to show me around your fabulous city. It was truly amazing to see it all," Livia said as she rushed back toward the steps.

"There's so much more I can show you."

"Oh, Adlar, I must go, my father will be wondering where I am."

"Then you must go. I can show you more of

the city another day."

"My father is an impatient man. I can't let him send people looking for me. He would be very angry."

"Goodbye Adlar, we'll see each other soon I hope," Livia said, leaning in and gave Adlar a soft kiss on the cheek and quickly ran off.

Adlar could not have caught up to her even if he wanted to. She left so abruptly that he was shocked more than anything. He felt a sudden urge of sadness. Adlar wasn't sure if he would ever see Livia again. He had already grown very fond of her in such a short time. Luckily, he knew that she could be found in the harbor. Adlar would have to wait a short while before he went back to the harbor. He was hoping to set sail to Tatilan soon, which is when he could see Livia again. Adlar wasn't sure if he even had time to spend with Livia before sailing out.

Adlar was very giddy and in awe over Livia as he walked to his room and sat down at his table. Adlar smiled as he thought about Livia's soft lips when she kissed him. She was different than any other woman he had ever seen or met. Adlar wished he ran after her back to the harbor. He was growing very impatient waiting for Theo and Tobias to return. Adlar stood and paced back and forth in his room for a minute. He strolled over to his bookshelf and grabbed his father's book. Adlar opened the large, untitled burgundy cover, sat, and began to read.

11th day of the 2nd Month of Spring of the 1194th Year

It has been quite the last couple weeks. Tymin and I just arrived back from the island of Rozann. I had a dream where I was on an island surrounded by tall mountains and dense forests. I heard whispers saying, "Come, come, come." It seemed too real to be a dream. I woke that morning and asked around if anyone knew of such an island. Sure, enough Tymin said he had heard rumors of an island which no one had ever been to before, just west of Raveria. My dream briefly showed war and destruction. I know war isn't upon us but, I took this as a sign to seek the island. I asked Tymin if he would come with me. Although we had never been, Tymin gladly agreed to accompany me. We arrived at the island quicker than expected. The fact that we had little idea of the islands whereabouts and found it so quickly was astounding. When we hit the shore, a group of strange looking men greeted us. They already knew our names, and I discovered that they were the ones talking to me in my dream. Remarkable, I thought. These men told us they were sorcerers, so it made some sense that they were able to talk to me through a dream, but how. We learnt that they had great power and ability to not only talk to the minds of anyone in Fallendor but also see into their minds. Although, the sorcerer's power could only be used on the island of Rozann. We had endless questions and thankfully we received an equal amount of answers. The leader of the sorcerers was Najal. He was a very short man with a slouched back and a short neck. He was an interesting man but spoke with so much wisdom. How couldn't he be so wise, he could see into everyone's mind. I had a thought that if I had such power what it would be like to look into the mind of Larrius. If he ever wanted to attack, I would know, and I could stop him. I asked Najal if he could help us. He wanted to pass on part of his powers to help but only if I brought my queen to the island. A sacrifice would have to be made. The sorcerer Najal told us that they were sent to the island from another world. However, their power was running out. The fuel to their power was a rare mineral on the island or the blood of a female no younger than eighteen. I could never bring my queen to the island as a sacrifice, my loving wife and dear queen, I could never. I lied to Najal that I would make such a sacrifice. This was to gain his trust and also gain the power of sight from him. Of course, I never followed through, how could I do such a thing. Najal took my crown anyways and casted some sort of magic upon it. This crown now gives me the power to see into the mind of any one enemy I want. As soon as I put on the crown, I saw my brother Larrius plotting to send his army north. I had to head back home to Mouro and send men to ambush the enemy. This crown is very important. The ability to see into the minds of my enemy will help us win the war. Najal made sure of it that I could use the crown in other places than Rozann. I can't tell anyone of this gift. We could be in danger if word gets out. I must go now. I have a war to win. Starian.

20th day of the 4th Month of Summer of the 1194th Year

He did it! Larrius attacked us! I never knew his jealousy would lead to this. I haven't been able to write because of the war. We won though; the War of Peace is what people are calling it. We suggest the peace and harmony built by my father before me was back. Larrius's Tatilinian troops were mostly depleted. However, my brother Larrius was able to escape in one piece. He won't be back though; I am certain of it this time. I had to leave my loving wife, and my dear queen who is pregnant with our first child. The baby is due soon, I would like to call the baby Adlar, if it's a boy. He was our bravest man on the battlefield. He fought courageously and slayed many enemies. He took an arrow to the back as the battle dwindled down. Not a pleasing sight to see. I hope my children will be as brave as he was one day. Starian.

    Adlar shook his head, trying to understand what he had read about the crown, and how it was extremely powerful. He knew that getting it back would be essential for his reign in Raveria. If in the wrong hands…he couldn't imagine.

Adlar was also surprised to learn about the sorcerer Najal and why they were on the island. He wondered why no one ever talked about them or knew of their existence. Adlar had no idea that his uncle Larrius was the one who waged war on the north. And because of jealousy and a title he wasn't given? King Starian made sure there was no ruler of Fallendor. This would have just brought on more conflict, especially with Larrius still at the helm in Tatilan. Adlar also found out that he was named after one of his father's greatest soldiers. He took great pride in that honor.

Perhaps his father and Tymin didn't want anyone to know. Adlar thought to himself that more than ever they had to move quickly and get his crown back. Just then, the city bells rang. It was Theo and Tobias, finally arriving in the capital. Adlar was excited to hear those bells ringing with positive meaning this time. Adlar bolted out of his chair and ran through the hallway, down the steps and toward the courtyard to greet his brother and Theo, the steward of Bedria. Theo and Tobias had returned much to Adlar's delight.

"Tobias, welcome back brother," Adlar said with open arms.

"Good to be back, brother," Tobias said.

"And Theo, good to see you again." Adlar

hugged the boys.

"I am so very proud of you being king of Raveria, I know it was your wish," Theo said. "Where is Agaras? I am going to kill him."

"Now hold up, I take it Tobias told you about your father, I am so sorry about this Theo," Adlar said, trying to console Theo. "I can take you to where your father was buried to say goodbye."

"I have already talked to Tobias about this on our journey, people die I know, but your brother Agaras is dead if he is found guilty," Theo explained, who now was calm.

Theo looked a lot like his father, with his dark brown eyes almost identical to Tymin's and his sandy blonde locks resembling his father's when he was at the same age. He also had a slight scar just under his left eye. Theo was a few years older than Adlar and Tobias and he had grown very close to the boys at a younger age when he lived in Mouro. He left the capital to become steward of Bedria and had governed the northern city for almost eleven years.

"It is so good to see you again Theo," Adlar admitted.

"I was reluctant to come back knowing my father was dead. But Tobias says we need to find Agaras to question him about his wrong doings," Theo said.

"We cannot assume our brother did this until we are certain," Tobias suggested.

"Boys it is so good to see you both again. Let

us leave this courtyard, there are far too many locals around. I must tell you something, follow me," Adlar said as he left for Theo and Tobias to follow behind.

They walked hastily and arrived by the pool in front of the king's Castle.

"Your father was right about the crown; it does have power. He told us this before he died," Adlar stated, now that he had quiet and privacy. "I have been reading my father's books, and I have learnt so much already. Things like who I was named after or why our uncle started the war which ended up being called the War of Peace. There are also sorcerers on an island that came from another world, it just doesn't make sense," he confessed calmly.

"But what about the crown?" Theo questioned.

"The crown was made powerful by a sorcerer named Najal. Our fathers went to Rozann, which apparently is just west of Proda," Adlar explained.

"They went because my father had a vision. Only later did he find out it was just Najal talking in his mind. Najal had the power to see into any mind in all of Fallendor, perhaps the same voice that Agaras said he heard. My father wanted an advantage if a war arose. Najal gave my father's crown power to see into the mind of his true enemy, our uncle Larrius. When my father used his crown, he saw Larrius and his men making their way north to attack Raveria, he learned of the Tatilinian army's plans and strategies. Father knew where to counterattack and wiped out most of the army. The battle for peace was won and no one has fought since," Adlar continued.

"So, Father kept this from us all along?" Tobias asked, confused.

"He must have known you would find out eventually," Theo said. "I never even knew my father accompanied him."

"We cannot let Larrius get the crown from Agaras. We have to set sail at sunrise tomorrow," Adlar explained.

King Adlar hoped they would make it south before Agaras arrived. If they did, they could agree with Larrius to banish Agaras for what he was thought to have done. Then they could get the crown back before Larrius could seize it. Luckily for Adlar the king in Tatilan did not know the power the crown held. King Larrius had his own crown; Adlar's crown had no value to him, unless Agaras revealed the secret of the crown. If King Larrius was to find out the power of the crown, it could be very dangerous for Fallendor. King Larrius had broken the first Treaty of Fallendor, so they had to assume he might do so again.

"Tobias, I want you to stay here in Mouro. Theo and I will travel with a group of men south."

"It might be a dangerous journey, so we need you to be in charge here in case anything happens to either of us. We need family here in the north so we can continue to reign," Adlar explained, as he led the boys up the steps of the king's castle to his room.

"Do I have to?" Tobias asked.

"I want to come. Please do not take this chance for adventure away from me!"

"I am sorry Tobias, but you must stay here." Adlar put his hand on Tobias's shoulder and empathized with his brother's hurt.

Tobias wasn't happy with this, but he felt a sense of honor about being left in charge. He thought now was the time to tell them what he knew.

"Agaras said he killed our father. He told me when I went looking for him."

"I couldn't believe him. I still don't, but I thought you both would want to know," Tobias quickly added.

"You ought to have told us this earlier," Adlar responded.

"Maybe that's why he left Father's room in such a hurry before. He was scared," Tobias said.

"How can this be? Perhaps it is true he killed my Father after all," Theo replied.

"We only think Agaras killed your father, and now that he may have killed our father as well. He also stole my crown. Where did things go wrong for Agaras? He was such a harmless quiet young boy. Were we too hard on him all these years?" Adlar pondered in sadness.

"We are not sure if he killed our father though. Or if he truly did kill Tymin. But we do know he has the crown and we have to find it and him. Then we can question him regarding these deaths,"

Tobias stated.

"Theo, come. We must depart, our crew and ship await us in the harbor. Tobias you are in charge. Farewell brother," Adlar said as he and Theo fled for the harbor.

Tobias followed them as far as the gate. He was disappointed in Adlar's wishes. Staying in Mouro and running things in his absence seemed to be a positive vote of confidence for someone as young as Tobias. The idea of not being able to use his abilities to fight if that ever was required on their journey was unfortunate for Tobias. He didn't want to stay in Mouro though. He thought, with Adlar and Theo gone, he could go anywhere he wished. Tobias watched them leave until they were out of sight. He packed some things to make his way to his new city, Proda. Tobias recalled that life was said to be great there. He would finally get a taste of the west coast. When his bags were ready, he carried them to the stables in search of a horse.

"May I borrow a horse, sir?" Tobias asked the stable hand.

"You don't need to ask. Do you not know who you are?" the man replied.

"Right, thank you."

"Where are you headed?" the man asked, taking the bags and loading them onto a large white steed.

"I am going to Proda. I am the new steward there!" Tobias said as he mounted the horse.

"I have heard wonderful things about Proda, I have family that live there. It is an easy ride there and back, too."

"I do not know when I will be back though. Farewell sir." Tobias bolted out of the stable and toward the road.

Tobias didn't care that much about what Adlar had asked of him. All he could think about was the island his father had gone to. Tobias didn't have a clue how someone would get there, but he did know Proda was the closest place to the island. He wanted adventure and perhaps now was his only opportunity. He wasn't going to let it go to waste. A cold wind brushed along his face as he started on his way to Proda and grey clouds came roaring in.

CHAPTER FIVE

Raveria normally enjoyed blue skies and beaming sunlight. For eight months of the year, the world of Fallendor had lovely summer temperatures. The second month of spring was coming to an end, and the first month of summer approached. Spring, however, was rougher than usual this year. There had never been as many torrential downpours before. As the Ruler of Raveria, King Adlar wished he could control the weather. However, it would be enough if the rain would just stop for a little while.

    Maxall had predicted a long voyage south in the sea. If it could just stop raining for a moment, it would make himself and Adlar and the entire crew much happier. The waters of the Grey Sea were said to be very rough waters which was one of the reasons why no one had ventured south before. A roar of thunder echoed so loud that all of Raveria would have heard it. It was time for King Adlar and his men to set sail. The crew was already at the harbor waiting for him and Theo to arrive. They were getting soaked in the rain and could not find any shelter to keep themselves dry. The streets of Adon Harbor, widely known for its usual buzzing and vibrant atmosphere, had been completely abandoned. The rain kept the people indoors. It was no surprise really; the rain was now pouring down in buckets. In a town that just yesterday was filled with so much life and excitement, all that could be heard now was the rain splashing into the large puddles that had quickly built up. Entering the harbor on his horse, Adlar reassured himself that no such rain could prevent him and his men from sailing south.

Adlar's drenched face depicted devastation. It was hard for anyone to look like they were enjoying this heavy downpour. He also knew Livia, the woman he had already grown fond of, lived in the harbor and hoped to see her before setting off on their journey. However, the dreary weather kept Livia away from her regular affairs in the harbor market. She was nowhere to be seen. Adlar's head dropped and stared into the puddles that had accumulated. His thoughts were clouded, his heart raced rapidly at the thought of Livia, but he had to continue on his quest.

Adlar thought he would see Livia again once he returned. There was no time to wait, as they had to set sail. King Adlar and Theo met with the group of men at the shoreline waiting to board the ship.

"Adlar sir, we have a problem," Maxall stuttered.

"What is it?" Adlar quickly replied.

"The ship, I miscalculated the wheel of the steer," Maxall said. "I tried turning it to test it in the water but it fell right off its axis."

"Well, can you fix this?"

"I can. But unfortunately, I have to wait until the rain stops so I can install dryer wood."

"What! It isn't supposed to stop raining for days!"

"I know my king. I am so sorry. It won't be fixed for another few days," Maxall said.

"However, I have a much smaller boat that should be strong enough to sail the Grey Sea," Maxall continued.

"Where is this boat?" Theo asked.

"It's in the bay. Ready to set sail. Thing is, you'll only be able to take a few men as it is much smaller," Maxall admitted.

"Very well. Theo and you five load the boat!" Adlar demanded. "The rest of you can head back to the city and get dry."

"Uh, Adlar. I have to come with you too. No one else really knows how to use my boat. It was my mistake. Let me come," Maxall suggested.

"Who will finish the ship?" Theo asked.

"Do not worry, you two. My younger brother

Densis is just as crafty as I am. I've already told him about my mistake, so he will fix the steer when the rains stop. If it stops," Maxall said. "My brother can even sail it too. When we get back let the young boy take you out for a spin in the sea."

"Alright. Let's go, we must hurry," Adlar demanded.

King Adlar, Theo, Maxall and five men set out to sea in Maxall's medium sized boat. Maxall's shoulders slumped, and his hollowed face appeared lifeless. He had been working on the king's ship for weeks. Maxall was a proud man but, he was devastated he broke the steer in the larger ship. This boat was much smaller than the ship King Adlar was hoping to take. It only had four beds snuggled close to each other and not much room for storage. It looked like if a heavy wave came crashing in, all the boat's substances would have lodged overboard. Maxall was at the back of the boat steering the crew out of the bay when he was joined by Adlar.

"My King, it's wonderful, isn't it?" Maxall said.

"I appreciate you coming along with us. Don't be so hard on yourself for breaking your own creation. We will get to Tatilan eventually," Adlar said.

"I assure you this boat will get us to Tatilan in one piece. If only it could keep us dry." Maxall replied, "Once my ship is ready to sail, we can explore more of Fallendor and travel way more efficiently."

"I have great faith that you will get us to Tatilan. All of Raveria depends on it," Adlar said as he gave one last look of disappointment to the harbor. He really had hoped to see Livia before he left.
The rain slowed down, as a delicate mist spewed from the dim clouds. Theo joined Maxall and King Adlar at the back of the boat.

"Do you know what you are doing Maxall?" Theo asked.

"Oh, come on, I got us out of the bay. I am an expert," Maxall replied with a sarcastic smile.

"Just make sure you get us there alive," Theo said as he slicked back his soaked locks.

"Why did you not tell us about this boat before?" Adlar said.

"Yeah. We could have found Agaras by now and could have given him what he deserves," Theo said, still disappointed to hear about his father.

"You never asked. You said you wanted a large ship. I always had this in the back of my mind as an alternative. All is well though," Maxall said.

"How long of a journey are we expecting Maxall?" Adlar asked.

"Could be a day, could be a week, who is to say. I have never done this before," Maxall replied.

"Ah great, wake me up when we get there," Theo blurted, annoyed with Maxall's estimate.

No one on board had ever sailed south through the Grey Sea before, so the length of journey was unknown to everyone. Theo made his way down to the smaller lower deck, kicked off his boots and hopped into a bed. There were two others laying down resting their eyes. It was now only King Adlar and Maxall up. Clouds were clearing and the rain had finally stopped. The ship was on its course to Tatilan.

"Let's hope the rain holds off for the rest of our journey," Adlar said, tilting his head up toward the grey skies. "It could be a long time before we arrive, we don't want a little rain taking us away from all the fun."

"Don't you worry my king; take a seat and we'll get there when we get there," Maxall insisted.

"Alright then, I need a drink, I will be back shortly," Adlar said as he walked away for a drink of ale.

Silence fell over the entire ship. Men were either sleeping or having a drink amongst themselves. It was dark out, so there wasn't much else the men could do but wait for their arrival. The chopping waters of the Grey Sea had finally settled. Calm waters would certainly make it easier on those that were sleeping. It also would make things a lot easier for Maxall to sail. Maxall had the ship at a steady pace. He was now the only one aboard that was awake, or at least it seemed that way. His gaze traced the starry night, and he sailed his way into the peaceful darkness.

Morning had come and the Grey Sea had a

grim blanket of fog over the calm waters. Thick misty clouds had appeared. So thick, that the thought of turning the boat around crossed Maxall's mind. King Adlar joined Maxall once again. He was one of the first persons awake. He usually was the first to rise for any occasion. However, it looked as if he hadn't got a wink of sleep all night. His hair was ragged, and his green eyes were weary.

"Smooth sail so far Maxall?" Adlar asked with a yawn.

"Of course, the stars kept me company all night and guided my way. This wild fog will be the death of us though," Maxall explained trying to swat away the fog with his hands.

They had no clue where exactly they even were, nor would they know when they would arrive in Tatilan. All they knew was Tatilan was the furthest point south, so were bound to hit it eventually.

"Maxall, perhaps once daylight breaks and the sky clears, we will be able to see land," King Adlar said as he now leaned up against the railing.

"Perhaps you are right my king, could you watch the steer for a moment? I must rest my legs for a while," Maxall asked. He had been standing since they left so his legs would have been exhausted. Maxall also didn't get any sleep, and everyone could tell by his haggard appearance.

"Certainly, my friend, you have taken us this far, let me take us the rest of the way," Adlar replied as if he knew what he was doing.

Maxall sat on the floor next to the king and fell instantly asleep.

"This is truly wonderful," Adlar said out loud to himself. "Me, the king, getting to steer a fancy boat. This is easier than I imagined, just standing here holding the wheel. I wonder what turning feels like. He jolted the boat to the left as he turned it off its original course.

The jolt woke up Maxall who was right next to Adlar.

"My king, what on earth are you doing?" Maxall said as he rushed to his feet to grab the steer.

"I was only having a bit of fun; we cannot see where we are going anyway," Adlar suggested pushing Maxall aside.

"You have altered our course, now I truly do not know where we are going," Maxall said, his voice laced with concern.

"Not that we knew where we were anyways," Adlar muttered under his breath.

Maxall was a proud serious man and rarely took kind to joking matters, even if it was his friend Adlar.

"Leave me to it, I need to focus on getting us back on course," Maxall said.

Before King Adlar could even leave, there was an enormous thump. Those who hadn't woken up yet were surely awake now. Another large thump occurred right afterwards. This time a large piece of wood was dislodged from the front of the boat.

A piece of the ship's siding fell off into the water.

"What the hell was that!" a frightened soldier yelled.

"Everybody, hold on!" Adlar shouted.

The boat had gained speed but was surely off its course now, the small sails and mast came crashing down after yet another thud. The ship crashed into rocks and it was tossed back and forth between two large cliffs. One of the crew members was launched overboard. The boat made its way several meters further before it came to a sudden stop. Everyone laid on the deck as they had taken cover. There was a large leak in the bottom of the boat and it slowly filled up with water. Soldiers scurried on to their feet and tried to bail the water out that was rushing in far too fast for anyone to stop the flow. The bashed up wooden boat creaked and shook as it started to sink.

"Men, we need to climb those cliffs," Theo shouted, as he noticed a way onto land.

The front half of the ship was smashed and buried into the dark rocks of the cliff. Men scattered to get climbing. Some men tried to grab as many supplies and weapons as they could. There was panic amongst everyone on the boat. Some men had no time to climb the cliffs as the entire boat was sinking fast, they jumped into the ice-cold water, the weight of the waves making it very hard to swim, not many knew how to swim, but determination rallied the men around to shore. The last soldier was able to climb up onto the cliff before the remains of the boat completely sunk into the depths of the sea. The other men that swam around were able to find a spot to climb up as well.

"Well, at least we made it," Theo said, beaten and bruised from being tossed around.

"Is everyone okay? Gather around here, we must regroup," King Adlar bellowed, as he was looking around wondering what had just happened. It did seem to be Adlar's fault in the first place, for turning the wheel to go off the course. Everyone was in disbelief and disarray. Maxall had been searching out into the water as he saw his boat disappear into the water. An opening of fog cleared as Maxall gazed out to sea.

"I do not think this is Tatilan, my king. I believe that is," he suggested, as he pointed off into the distance.

A massive bit of land bordered the entire horizon, Maxall was certain it was Tatilan.

"So, you are saying we are stranded on this island, with no ship, very few supplies and the very place we got to be is miles that way?" Adlar said with anger in his voice.

"It seems as if we are quite a long way away now. The nation of Tatilan covers all the south, the size of that land over there makes perfect sense that that's where we should be," Maxall explained.

"So, we are trapped, great," Theo yelled, as he tossed his helmet to the ground in anger.

"You might need that," Adlar said with worry in his voice.

"I won't need my helmet if I am on this lifeless dump," Theo sighed.

No one knew the place they had been shipwrecked on. The island appeared to be just north of Tatilan so King Adlar and his crew were just off its course. They had no way of even getting there from this distance. Swimming was not an option because it was too far and most of the crew couldn't even swim. All they could do was wait until rescue came for them, but that could take weeks before someone notices where they are. This island was where they would have to make their home for the time being. Its shores were sheer rock, but there were plenty of trees to protect them from the sun. Lots of trees for the men to perhaps build a boat that could get some men across the channel to Tatilan and get help.

"Everyone, let's get settled in," King Adlar suggested. "We can explore this island's forests. See if we can find any food. We can use the wood from these trees to build a boat. We are lucky to have Maxall the craftsman amongst us, he can certainly build something for us to get off this rock."

"If anyone wants to explore the island with me, come follow me," Theo said as he started walking toward the trees.

A loud mysterious noise came out of the dark forest. Everyone gasped in fear and panic. Theo was closest to the deep howl.

He looked back toward the group of men. "We are not alone!"

Another roar came from the dense darkness from the forest. The men on the island were all looking amongst each other confused and frightened.

"Men, something might be coming," Theo stated.

"Whatever comes out we must stand strong. Theo get back!" Adlar yelled, as there was a rustle in the forest.

The men were without a lot of their weapons and equipment that had sunk with the boat. Everyone was able to find a piece of weaponry to aid them if something came from the bushes. They had no clue what was making such noise.

"Can anyone see what it is?" Adlar yelled.

"I don't want to get too close." A soldier stepped back.

A large beast slowly came roaring out from the bushes, before its pace quickened like a hurricane blistering through a village. The beast was several feet long and had razor sharp teeth. Its teeth appeared to have the strength to bite through stone. Its head had spiraled horns on either side and a long-pointed snout. A few arrows were fired by soldiers which barely penetrated the beast's charcoal brown-colored fur.

This creature's speed and aggression was enough to dislodge any arrows that did connect to its hide. Maxall had a spear and threw it toward the beast which pierced its back. The beast let off a terrorizing roar, which only agitated it more. The beast sprinted toward Maxall and a couple soldiers tried to stand in its way. The beast launched two soldiers many yards into the air. Maxall was unarmed and too slow to grab his dagger to protect himself. Maxall was thrown to the ground and the beast started to maul his face with its teeth and razor claws. Blood splattered out from Maxall's face as the beast ripped a huge chunk of skin off his face with ease. Maxall was unrecognizable, only his curly dark hair showed as he was breathless.

"NO!" Adlar yelled.

Adlar shook from seeing his dear friend get mauled by the behemoth beast. No one had ever seen such a ruthless creature before. King Adlar and Theo were far enough from the beast but could still see what was going on. There were only three men that stood in between them and the beast. The creature slowly approached the group of men with blood from Maxall dripping from its dark fur. Waiting for the beast to make a move, Adlar grabbed a spear and tossed it in its direction. The spear landed in the beast's right shoulder forcing it to limp as it walked closer to the group. The beast gave off another large howl in pain, but remained unfazed by the spear in its shoulder. The men courageously made a move and charged the beasts with swords and spears. The beast was no match, as one by one it knocked the soldiers to the ground with its large horns. Then ripped the three soldiers open to their death. Adlar and Theo now had a standoff with the large unknown creature as they remained the last two alive. The beast was hungry for more blood and wanted it's last two victims. The beast's yellowish eyes pierced right through Adlar, as the two stared at each other. Adlar maintained eye contact and signaled Theo to go behind the beast. Theo slowly made his way around the beast and prepared to attack it. Simultaneously the brothers and the creature attacked.

The beast's massive claw barely missed Adlar's face but connected to his shoulder, sending him to the ground. Theo jumped at the beast and lodged his sword deep into the it's back. The beast let off a scream of pain and anger. Theo was now unarmed as the beast tossed him near Adlar and approached them. The beast wanted to finish off Adlar and Theo. Before the beast had the chance, Adlar quickly rolled over and grabbed a spear that was laying amongst the dead bodies. Adlar picked the spear up with his uninjured arm and stabbed it through the neck of the beast. The beast shrieked and fell to the ground. The beast was motionless and its yellow eyes of terror closed.

"What a mess," Theo said as he observed the dead bodies that surrounded himself and Adlar.

"We have to get off this island before another beast comes," Adlar replied.

"Where did that thing come from? I have never seen one before," Theo mentioned.

"Nor have I. It is a good thing too, that beast was the biggest thing I have ever seen," Adlar replied.

"I am sure it is just another secret our fathers kept from us," Theo said, sarcastically.

"I knew animals and beasts existed. But that thing was much too large to be anything that I know of."

"We should clean up the bodies and give them a proper goodbye."

"You are right. Can we do Maxall last? I want to say goodbye to my dear old friend."

"Of course, my king. Then we can figure out how we are going to get off this wretched rock."

Adlar and Theo would be saying goodbye to the men they just lost for the remainder of the day. They had to build some sort of shelter as well. They didn't know how long they would be on the island nor, did they know if any other beasts or creatures would come lurking for blood. The two were drained and wounded and didn't know if they could survive in such a deserted place for much longer.

they disappeared. Agaras felt a hard smack to the side of his head. Agaras was cranked in the head with a giant stick. Agaras fell to the ground and the three men started kicking him in the head and stomped on his stomach. Agaras laid on the ground defenseless as he covered his already dirty face with his hands. The three men each gave one last kick at Agaras and they left as they laughed and mocked him.

"Take me to Tatilan. What a fool," they said.

The three men laughed as Agaras stayed down coughing up blood. Agaras tried to pick himself up and struggled, as he was certain one of his ribs must have been broken. Agaras rolled around in pain and let out a yell of distress. He used a stick to pick himself up, the same stick that the men used to beat him. Agaras forced himself to his feet with all his strength and leaned up against a tree stump to catch his breath. He looked along the ground, and his belongings were scattered. Agaras hectically searched the bushes but couldn't find the crown. Agaras sighed in disbelief and pain. He thought for sure the men took it back to the pub. Agaras needed that crown if he was to go to Tatilan.

He came all this way just to get beaten up by three old men. He laughed in his mind. Agaras knew the men were bigger and older than him but, he had to do whatever he could to get the crown back. Agaras marched himself back into the village and straight to the local pub hoping to find the same three men. When Agaras walked in the front door they were nowhere to be seen.

"Those three men that were sitting over there. Did they come back this way?" Agaras asked the bartender.

"I am sorry but, I have not seen them since you guys left," the bartender kindly replied.

Agaras heard his horse neigh. He limped outside and saw the three men whacking his horse with long branches. "Hey, you! Stop, that is my horse," he demanded.

The three men stopped what they were doing and were surprised to see Agaras.

"How are you not dead, boy," the man with the scar said.

"You have something of mine. I want it back!" Agaras shouted as he approached the men.

"What, this?" the tall man said as he pulled out the crown.

"Yes, that is mine," Agaras replied.

"It is ours now," the other man said as he whacked the horse once more and it fled away from the village.

Agaras was sick of being antagonized, so he pulled out his knife and pointed it toward the men. "I have already used this on someone who has got in my way. I am not afraid to use it again," he threatened.

The three men laughed hysterically. Agaras in one swift blow swung his knife so fast he sliced two of the men's throats. They fell to the ground. The man with the scar looked up and was shocked. Blood pooling out on the ground. Turning the lush grass red.

"Here, have the crown. You crazy," the scarred man said, handing the crown over to Agaras. Blood covered Agaras' face. It was uncertain if it was still his own blood from getting beaten or blood from the men he just killed.

"Thank you," Agaras said and murdered the man just like the other two.

The man with the scar fell to the ground like a rock in a puddle.

"Hey, someone call for help! Alert the guards!" a lady yelled from back into the village.

Agaras knew that he had just been seen murdering three men, so he ran as fast as he could back to the shore. Agaras forgot he had even been beaten and was running with no limp in his step. He sprinted so fast through the village and toward the shore. He started pushing the small wooden boat into the water. Agaras had no idea how to paddle a boat but knew he had to try or he would be arrested. He quickly washed off the blood and dirt from his face. Agaras heard yells and people running around in the village. He hopped in the small wooden boat and wobbled away in the water. People appeared from the bushes just as he was out of range.

"That is the man who killed them," the woman said to two soldiers on horseback.

"If the waters do not finish him, then those in Tatilan will. Leave him be," the horseman said.

Agaras was relieved. He could see land

approaching as the waves carried him closer. Agaras noticed the waves leading him straight to what he believed was Tatilan. He put his head on the side of the boat and rested his eyes.

"Ay, get up. What are you doing here?" a farmer said, waking up Agaras.
Agaras was confused as ever as he had fallen asleep. He was at a shore now and a farmer was poking his face with what looked like a stick to herd cattle. "I am sorry sir. Is this Tatilan?"

"Well of course, where else would it be," the farmer said.

"Is the King of this place around? I need to speak with him," Agaras asked.

"Well boy. Tapura is where he would be. He does not take kindly to visitors. Even the people that live in his city revolt, interfering with his daily routine. Come to think of it though lad, no one has any idea what he even does in his castle. It is so large no one ever sees him," the farmer continued.

"Where can I find Tapura?" Agaras asked as he jumped out of the boat and onto the sandy shore.

"Well you see, it is right up the road. Once you get to the hill way over there you should be able to see a large city," the farmer said. His pointy red nose and round cheeks shook every time he spoke. The farmer was quite short and stout, but Agaras thought he was a rather wholesome person.

"Thank you, kind sir," Agaras said.

"Where are you from?" the farmer asked after Agaras grabbed his things and made his way for the hill.

Agaras didn't turn around to answer the man. He thought he shouldn't let people know he's from Raveria. Agaras limped again as he made his way over the hill and the farmer was right. As soon as he got over the hill a huge city appeared before his eyes. At first Agaras thought the city was a rather grotesque place. When he cleared his eyes and looked closer, he noticed the beautiful limestone walls of the city shimmering in the southern sunshine. Tatilan was highly known for its stunning architecture and massive cities and castles. Tatilan was large and its mountains were filled with limestones and other materials Raveria or Azden did not have. The city Tapura was the capital and was where the King of Tatilan lived. Agaras heard a voice in his head say, "You've made it, you are home."

Agaras stopped walking, confused. He scanned around him and didn't see anyone nearby that could have been talking to him. Agaras thought to himself that he hadn't heard this voice in his head since the day his father died. So, he was even more confused but Agaras knew he had to keep moving.

Agaras arrived at the front gate of Tapura, he was amazed by the beauty of the city walls, sparkling like stars in the night sky. He was unaware of the reception he would get when he entered the city. He never met his uncle but what he learnt from stories was he was never an easy man to please. Any arrival of a stranger would have gone unwanted by the King of the South, which is what the farmer Agaras met said.

Agaras was halted at the gate by some city guards.

"Do not get any further," one guard demanded.

"Stop walking now," another guard said as he drew an arrow from his back and aimed it at Agaras.

"I mean no harm. I wish to see your King," Agaras said.

"King Larrius does not see visitors. Leave now," the guard said.

"Can you tell King Larrius then that, his nephew is here and has the crown of Raveria," Agaras said.

The guards looked back at each other and one left quickly back into the city and the other ordered the gate to open.

Agaras was not surprised as he entered the city that all of the people were staring at him. He was left speechless at the stunning pillars and buildings within the walls. Even the cobblestone roads were something to be amazed by.

A crowd gathered beneath a large set of steps. Agaras couldn't see what was up the steps but he did notice a precession of people making their way down the steps. To Agaras, it seemed that it may have been the king making his way to the city square below the steps. Agaras quickly walked over to the people and was waiting for the crowds to clear for the king.

King Larrius was very tall in stature and had dark eyes, dark hair and pale skin. He had a look on his face as if he did not know how to be happy. It was no wonder he didn't like any visitors but, who would want to visit such a man Agaras thought.

"What brings you to my city scum?" King Larrius asked in a raspy voice.

"I am Agaras. I am your brother's youngest son," Agaras replied and was frightened.

"I said, what are you doing here?" Larrius asked again.

"I have come to tell you that your brother is dead," Agaras stammered.

"You came all this way to tell me that my brother is dead? He was dead to me years ago when I was sent here," Larrius said.

"Were you banished?" Agaras quietly asked.

"Do not ask me questions boy!" King Larrius yelled back. His dark eyes got darker the angrier he became.

"I brought you this crown," Agaras said as he lifted the crown up for all to see.

"I do not need a crown, silly boy. I have my own, keep that for yourself," Larrius suggested.

"But, uncle, this crown is now my brother Adlar's he is king of Raveria, the same one my father wore before," Agaras replied.

"You stole your dead father's crown from

your brother that is truly the best news I have heard in years," King Larrius said in disgust at the very mention of his older brother.

"My father did not want me to be King of Raveria. He loved my other brothers above me. I never wanted to be a steward, so I left," Agaras said.

"People of Tapura. Please leave us be. Leave us!" Larrius shouted to the people.

They looked frightened every time he spoke so the people of this beautiful city went back to their daily lives.

King Larrius approached Agaras and put his hand on his shoulder. "Let's go up these steps where we can get away from the noise," the king said as he turned around to lead Agaras back up the steps. When they arrived at the top there were two large steps that entered into a large building. Agaras thought to himself that that must be where the King spends all his days.

"My dear boy, you want to be king right? Then be king, put on the crown and people will respect you," Larrius said.

"Not in Raveria they won't. My father was foolish not to make me king. He was confused during his last few days alive," Agaras replied.

"Why did you steal the crown and bring it to me?" King Larrius asked.

"The crown has power! I desired it, but I have not tried on the crown for myself. I wanted you to see for yourself, to show my respects and loyalty to you, my king," Agaras said.

"I think you should do it first boy. Put on the crown and see what happens," Larrius said.

Agaras without hesitation put on the crown of Raveria. He was jerked back a bit and slightly stunned.

"What is it?" King Larrius asked.

"I saw my brother Tobias. He was in the city Proda where we both were due to be stewards. Of course, the people were chanting his name and welcoming him with open arms. They never would've given me that reception," Agaras replied with an unhappy look on his face as he took off the crown. Agaras handed it to Larrius to put on to see if he could see what he saw. Larrius took off his own crown and put on the crown of Raveria. King Larrius jolted back as well.

"Did you see something too?" Agaras was quick to ask.

"I saw two men on an island, it looked as if they were in distress," King Larrius replied.

"Who were they? Did they look like they were from the north?" Agaras asked.

"They did look foreign to me. Quite similar to yourself come to think of it. They did look Raverian," Larrius said. "Tell me Agaras, do you know what your people would be doing washed up on an island for?"

"Uh, perhaps they are looking for this crown that I stole, perhaps my brother Adlar wants it back."

"I used to spy on my father. He said one day that the crown allowed him the ability to see into your mind. That is how he was able to defeat you during the War of peace."

"I knew our defeat was unexpected. My brother was scared of me so he had to use dark powers to defeat me," Larrius said with a crooked smile.

"What did the men you saw look like uncle?" Agaras asked.

"One man was tall and had a reddish-brown beard and slicked back dark hair," Larrius remembered.

"That sounds a lot like my brother Adlar, the new king of Raveria," Agaras interrupted Larrius before hearing about the other.

"Any king in the north will be an enemy of mine, I am glad I can see he's in distress," Larrius admitted.

"Where are they though?" Agaras asked.

"There is an island just north of here called Demar. Few have even been there. It's said that a dangerous wild animal roam there. I have never been there before myself, but if that is where they are then they won't last long. However, my boy, it is curious as to why they were so far south. Since the War of Peace, we have had a treaty that states there would be no war. Perhaps your brother wants his crown back and attacking us was the only way."

"I think you are right, my brother wanted to

come here and attack Tatilan. He wanted to break the treaty to get the crown back."

"I will bring war back to Raveria if that's what they want. They are without their King."

"Manum, come here at once," King Larrius yelled.

A tall young man with olive skin and dark hair came running over.

"Manum, this is Agaras. Your cousin. I am making him captain of infantry for my army," Larrius stated.

"I never knew I had a cousin," Manum said, while stretching out his hand to shake Agaras'.

"Manum bring your assassins to Demar. There are two Raverian men looking to murder me there. One is the new king of Raveria. Kill him, bring back the other as our prisoner," Larrius said.

"Of course, father. I won't return until the king is dead." Manum marched off, confidently.

"If your brother is not killed by possible beasts on Demar. Manum and his group of assassins will finish him off, along with his companion," King Larrius demanded.

"What should we do?" Agaras asked.

"My dear boy, let me welcome you to Tapura, with my guidance we will march north and destroy Azden before we make it to Raveria and whip them all out. We will rule Fallendor together and get revenge on your father and brother's for treating you poorly."

"Yes, let us head north," Agaras said as he felt love from Larrius. Love he had not felt almost his whole life from his own family.

"First you must bathe. You are injured and filthy and it could be a long war, go at once," Larrius said as he called for a servant to assist Agaras. The servant guided Agaras to his bath.

"I shall see you tomorrow my boy, my queen awaits me in my chambers," King Larrius said. Larrius made way back to his room with the crown of Raveria still in his hand and a smile of joy on his face.

CHAPTER SEVEN

Proda was a lively and luxurious city, close to the west coast of Raveria. The people of Proda lived a rather lavish lifestyle, and it was one of the wealthiest cities in all of Fallendor. Its lands and mountains were known for their minerals, and these were mined minerals and sold to Mouro blacksmiths, as Mouro was known for smithing. With the mining of rich minerals, as well as their fishing, which they sold to the capital, Proda became a majorly wealthy city.

Tobias was finding out how great the people here were and had received a warm welcome from the citizens of Proda. It was expected that Agaras too would be arriving and this joy from the western lands of Raveria showed how excited the people were to have a new steward. Tobias was already making himself at home as steward, and had almost forgotten his brother Adlar had asked him to stay in Mouro while they were gone. Tobias didn't care. He'd finally got to meet his cousin Byrim, who had never wanted to be a steward and so he happily accepted Tobias's arrival.

As always, the city of Proda shone. This part of Raveria certainly enjoyed the sunshine, which the citizens saw all year round, even during the spring and winter months. The first day of the first month of summer had finally come, so it was no wonder Tobias followed the others and enjoyed the outdoors. Tobias was leaning up against the entrance way to the yard where knights were training. Byrim and Tobias were making friendly bets as to which soldier was the better fighter. The sun was glowing off the walls, forcing Tobias and Byrim to shield their eyes.

"My money is on the tall lad," Byrim said.

"I guess I am losing this bet," Tobias said as he noticed the opponent was almost half everyone's size.

Tobias and Byrim watched on as the other soldiers gathered around. Byrim was a couple years older than Tobias, and there was no question he was a relative of Tobias; they had the same hazel eyes. Although Tobias was rather tall for a nineteen-year-old, Byrim stood even taller than he did. He was a handsome young man with finely trimmed brown hair and a smile that charmed all.

The crowd cheered, as the duel waged on.

A bystander yelled at the smaller short fighter, "You do not stand a chance."

The two fighters were only training but, were going all out, much to the delight of those watching. Swords swung back and forth, as clouds of dirt filled the air with their every move. The taller and much broader fighter was angry because the smaller opponent was winning. Tobias was shielding his eyes from the sun as he tried to figure out who the little fighter was but a full helmet covered their face, and he couldn't make it out.

"Looks like the little boy will be winning after all," Tobias said to Byrim joking.

"I do not understand how someone so large can get outdueled and out classed by such a small little man," Byrim said as they watched on.

The taller soldier was disarmed and lost the duel and he let out an angry grunt as he stormed off. The other knights cheered for the small underdog, and Tobias wanted to congratulate the victor.

"You there, congrats on your victory. That was quite the show, young boy," Tobias said.

"I am not a boy." A quiet voice sounded as the victor took off their helmet.

It was a young woman. Her long dark hair fluttered in the wind as she took off her helmet, catching the eye of both Byrim and Tobias. They looked at each other in shock.

"Are you guys going to say anything else or can I go wash up," the girl asked.

"Uh, I am sorry I just thought…" Tobias said.

"How long have you been training with us?" Byrim interrupted.

"Over a week now. My father never wanted me to be a knight, never thought there was a need for soldiers or knights, as Fallendor has been at peace for as long as I have been alive. I love swinging a sword though," the girl stated this with charm, which Tobias realized in her smile.

"What's your name," Tobias asked.

"My name is Sabina. You do not have to tell me yours; I know you are the new steward, I was at your welcoming Tobias," Sabina said.
A knight yelled from behind them. "She has been kicking our arses all week too."

"I've never seen anyone with such skill with a blade," said Byrim, explaining his expression of incredulity.

"Thanks. I met you a week ago Byrim. Thanks for remembering me," Sabina said as she polished her sword with a cloth she had pulled from a back pocket.

"Can I also say, wow you have got such beauty," Tobias gushed nervously.

"I do not have time to be gawked at by any young man. My focus is fighting for Raveria if the time arises," she said.

"Do you like adventure, Sabina?" Tobias asked

"Of course, I do," Sabina replied.

"Then come with me, I have an adventure for

us, I've been waiting for someone like you to accompany me," Tobias said.

"Can I at least wash up?" she asked as they started to leave the training yard.

"Uh, we should not be too long," Tobias said.

"What are you talking about Tobias?" Byrim asked.

"Byrim I think you should stay here. We are leaving but I hope to be back soon,"

Tobias said by way of explanation, obviously in a hurry.

Byrim was confused as was Sabina, but left the two be and walked away into the busy city streets.

Tobias led Sabina to the stable which gave off a nasty stench much to their displeasure.

"You want me to shovel horse shit, do you? I am not doing peasants work. I know you have people that serve you to do that," Sabina said in disgust.

"No, no. We need a horse for where we are going," Tobias said. "Listen, I can tell you more later. I need someone like you, who is also a good fighter."

"Oh, you are a good fighter like me? I doubt that," Sabina said as they prepared the horses. Tobias insisted "We do not have time to argue. We have to be back before my older brother returns to Mouro, because I was supposed to stay there."

"Sure. Why not. I live for adventure with our strange new steward of Proda," Sabina replied.

The two hopped on their horses and left the city.

"Where are we even going," Sabina asked.

"An island called Rozann. My father has been there. Apparently, there are powerful people there who can help me."

"Powerful people? How powerful?"

"They made the crown my father wore powerful. Last night in a dream I saw my mother on the island. I am not crazy but I think she told me to go to the place my father went," Tobias said. "Only thing is, I never met my mother so this could all be in my head."

"Well lucky for you, I know how to paddle a boat so I can help us get there. I have never been before but my Father taught me when I was younger. We went fishing from time to time."

The two arrived at the shoreline quicker than Tobias thought and pulled a boat off the land and into the water.

"Where are you taking that?" asked a man on the coast. It appeared he owned the few boats placed along the beach.

"We will not be long I promise. We have to be back soon for the new king of Raveria, which I fear could be in a day or two," Tobias explained as if it was already too late to turn back, although they were only a few feet away.

"Let's hope this boat floats," Sabina said.

Sabina and Tobias made their way across the gleaming sea, the waters were rougher as they got further out into the sea. The journey would not take long and the island had already started to appear on the horizon. Yet, it was still a decent distance away, as the current pulling against the boat slowed them down.

"So, you mentioned your father did not like the idea of you being a knight. How did you find the chance to fight and where is your father now?" Tobias asked once they finally figured out where they were steering.

"Well my mother spent a lot of time out late drinking. Some nights she wouldn't even come home. My father hated my mother's drinking addictions as much as I did. He scooped me up when I was four and brought us to Proda." Sabina's face fell as she recalled that time.

"I was born in Bedria. My father was overly protective and he wanted to protect me from my mother, so that is why we left when I was so young. He died fighting in the war though. A few years after arriving in Proda we learned my mother had died of alcohol poisoning. I have been alone in Proda for over fifteen years now. Having to fend for myself, no parents, no siblings, no friends. I snagged a sword off a guard because that was the only way I believed I could protect myself. I taught myself how to swing a sword, and spent many hours hacking away at trees and such. It was a troubling childhood but fighting brought me peace and allowed me to protect myself. I've had a hard life so far, but I am alive so that's all that matters now."

"I am so sorry. Have you just recently joined the Proda military?" Tobias asked.

"Do not feel bad for me we have all gone through things. But yes, I was finally able to sneak my way into the military over a week ago. They did not think it was appropriate to have a female amongst their ranks."

"Well I am glad I met you. I think we can be friends," Tobias said smiling.

"I think you are right. You seem less strange now," Sabina replied, smiling back.

"Look, we're almost there!"

Tobias and Sabina had been talking for a while and had lost track of time but they were now quickly approaching the shore of Rozann and managed to steer the boat right on to the beach. The two were instantly greeted by the sorcerers who lived on the island, appearing out of nowhere.

"What brings you two to the island of Rozann?" asked the leader of the group.

"You know my father Starian. His crown was stolen, and I was hoping you could help us," Tobias stated his intentions firmly.

"Until the crown is destroyed, or the king who possesses it dies, the power will remain, and we cannot give any power to another crown," the old man said.

There were five in all, all wearing black cloaks with hoods that almost covered their whole face.

"My name is Najal. I am the leader here on the island," said the leader. Then Najal explained.

"But, come. Let us welcome you properly."

Tobias hopped out of the boat first, landing onto the sandy shore, then he helped Sabina down as well. The island had looked baron from afar, but was packed with vibrant forests and flowers. Its mountains were tall and white as snow.

The group of hooded men accompanied Sabina and Tobias, leading them to their small village consisting of little huts made from wood and branches. Tobias found it curious and wondered, how in the world anyone could even live in such conditions, so secluded from the rest of Fallendor.

"What is your name boy?" Najal asked as they sat down by a crackling fire.

"My name is Tobias, steward of Proda," Tobias replied.

"And you are?" Najal asked, then looking toward Sabina, started whispering to the man beside him. Tobias and Sabina made eye contact, confused about what was going on.

"I am Sabina," she said slowly.

"So, what happened to your father?" Najal asked Tobias.

"My brother Agaras said he murdered him," Tobias replied.

"Such a pity," Najal said.

"How do you know so much?" Sabina asked.

"We sorcerers were given a gift, which we

were born with. We can see into people's minds. We know everything that happens in this world through the power of sight," Najal admitted.

"We were brought here from another world to observe Fallendor," another sorcerer said.

"When our gift was discovered by others, we were banished, if you could call it that. More like trapped prisoners of this island. We have been here for almost fifty years. We were told we could go back to our own world, but we would lose our gift, as we only now have such power on the island now," Najal explained.

Tobias and Sabina looked at each other and you could tell they had a million questions, but the sorcerers continued to speak.

"We discovered the source of our power, but we are running out of its fuel. So if you can help us, we will help you," Najal said.

"We want you to help us," Tobias said as he was handed a cup of soup that one of the men had been cooking over the fire.

"Up that mountain there is a beast. Far too strong and powerful for any of us. These beasts are found all over the World of Fallendor. They are called arivuk's and they roam island's and seek blood. One arivuk blocks the tunnel to the other side of this island. We have been trapped on this side of the island for a long time. If you can defeat the arivuk,

we will give you the same power we gave your father. We will give your sword the power of sight," Najal explained

"Arivuk's? What are they?" Sabina asked.

"They are vicious creatures that will kill anything that it lays its eyes on," a sorcerer explained.

"How exciting," Sabina sarcastically said.

"Now go that way up the mountain, both of you go, you will need all the help you can get," Najal said as he sent Tobias and Sabina out on their way up the path.

Rozann was an island of all sorts of natural aspects to it. Parts of it were shadowed by tall dense forests and other parts were barren and desert like. Then other parts of it had an abundant array of bright flowers shining in the light. The path leading up the mountain was dusty, but easy to walk on. Tobias and Sabina wished the trail was like that the whole way up, but it was not at all. A few minutes up the path ended and it became a steep cliff making it difficult to climb, although there were steps for them. Sabina, who spent a lot of her childhood climbing trees was experienced so was quicker than Tobias to climb. As they climbed the slick rock, they could no longer see the ground. The rocks were damp from the early morning rainfall that hit the island. This made it difficult for the two to climb, especially for Tobias who wasn't much of a climber. He needed Sabina's help multiple times. The top of the mountain was now in their sights. The climb at first looked more difficult than it turned out to be, much to the delight of Tobias and Sabina who weren't expecting to have to climb up a mountain. The two of them were able to use their strength and climb quicker now. Even though they knew uncertain danger was upon them Tobias knew this had to be done. Tobias and Sabina finally arrived at the top of the mountain and found a flat place to finally allow them to stand with safety. As soon as they stood up, the wind picked up as they approached a tunnel which they assumed was where the beast roamed. There was a tunnel that led to the other side of the island, the beast lived in a cave that was attached to this tunnel. Tobias and Sabina thought about how any beast could get on this island, but they also wondered what the sorcerers were doing on this island as well. A loud grumble came from the darkness of the cave as Tobias and Sabina quickly pulled out their swords. Their eyes widened as the wind blew up dust from off the cliffs.

"Sabina, stay put and I will lure the arivuk out here," Tobias whispered as he slowly entered the tunnel.

Sabina didn't seem to want to leave Tobias, but she left the tunnel to stand back outside. Tobias continued cautiously through the dark tunnel unaware if the beast would jump out to attack. He couldn't hear any more signs of the beast. Sweat started to fall down Tobias' forehead as he stood nervously in quiet. Not a sound could be heard, but Tobias could see a small sparkle of light peering from the end of the cave. The light went away and was now blocked by a large figure which gave off a loud roar. Tobias was so frightened by the noise that he fell off his feet. He scrambled to pick himself back up on his feet. Tobias was startled but was able to get up and run out of the cave. The beast could be heard slowly coming out of the tunnel as Tobias met Sabina back outside the cave.

"It is coming!" Tobias shouted.

Himself and Sabina had their swords ready for the beast to emerge. There was a moment of silence as the two waited. The large arivuk came rushing out from the cave. It gave off a huge roar and it slowly approached them. Tobias and Sabina separated themselves as the beast roared once again. Its teeth were the size of daggers. The eyes of the beast glowed yellow when the sunlight beamed into them. The beast rushed toward Tobias first and he was able to dodge the on-rushing beast. Sabina was quick to pierce the arivuk in its back. She was surprised its dark fur wasn't as strong as it may have first appeared. She took out the sword and stabbed the beast again, this time in the leg. The arivuk turned around in pain and clawed Sabina to the ground. She was severely winded and stayed down on the ground gasping for air. The beast was injured from the stab wounds, but the arivuk, now had Tobias in its sights. Tobias swung his sword at the beast's head which was deflected off the arivuk's large horns. The strength of the beast's bite was able to quickly clamp down on his blade. The blade was thrown by the beast toward Sabina. Tobias was now unarmed with all but a small shield as the arivuk knocked him to the ground. The beast was just about to make Tobias its lunch when it unexpectedly collapsed. Sabina placed both her own and Tobias' sword into the back of the arivuk and it fell to its death.

"How did you do that?" Tobias questioned, still in shock and fear.

"You mean, thank you?" Sabina replied.

"Not much of a beast," Tobias joked, trying to catch his breath.

"Easy for you to say," Sabina quickly replied.

"Alright let's climb back down and get the hell out of here, those guys creep me out," Sabina suggested.

"Just wait, I saw something back in the cave. I want to check it out, you go ahead," Tobias admitted.

"Suit yourself," Sabina said as she threw Tobias sword back to him and she began to climb down.

Tobias went to the cave. Curious to see what the sparkling light from the end of the tunnel was. He had thought it was just to the other side, but its glow made him want to take a second look. Tobias was thrilled he went back, as he saw a shining jewel. He rushed inside the cave to grab the jewel. He was amazed with the stone's beauty. He thought to himself that this may be a special jewel, so he wasn't going to tell anyone. Tobias felt something when he held onto it. Tobias tucked away the jewel to keep hidden. He thought to himself this was for sure what

Najal and the sorcerer's wanted. The beauty of the jewel made Tobias want to keep it for himself. He quickly left the cave. He felt the cool wind on his face once more as he ascended down the mountain to catch up to Sabina.

CHAPTER EIGHT

The mountain loomed over Tobias as he stumbled over jagged outcrops. He slipped on wet rock, falling against bushes and wincing as branches scraped his battered face. Breathing heavily, he steadied himself against a rock then sagged onto it.

Smoke rose from the village below. Not far to go—hopefully Sabina made it—she must have he thought. She did leave first after all. Tobias shuddered. He could still feel the beast's hot breath on his neck just before Sabina killed it—he owed her his life.

He opened the pouch at his waist and tipped a jewel into his palm. Faint sunlight caught a myriad of colors in the facets enhancing its beauty. But what's its purpose? Perhaps the sorcerers could tell them why the arivuk beast guarded it so ferociously. He rose wearily, even his bones ached.

The sweet perfume of flowers filled his nostrils as he walked between the village toward the fireplace. Sabina sat at a fire with the sorcerers, and relief flooded him.

She glanced up, small even teeth flashing in a grin. "You're slow." Her green eyes sparkled as they swept over him. "But then I guess you got beat up and I did not." Brushing a strand of black hair behind an ear, she waved a slim hand. "I am listening to stories. Sit."

He sank onto a log, then a blast of thick, black smoke enveloped him. Reeling, he coughed and rubbed his eyes.

Sabina chuckled.

He stared at her through a blur. "So, that was funny?" She nodded, smiling broadly. But the sorcerer' faces were like granite, their eyes fixed on him. What now? He controlled the coughing and wiped his eyes. "I am sure Sabina told you we killed the beast."

The oldest sorcerer, Najal smiled wryly. "It is our understanding that Sabina killed it."

Tobias nodded. "She did, but what matters is that you said if we kill the beast guarding the tunnel you would help us."

"Correct, Steward of Proda." Najal held out a bony hand. "Give me your sword."

Hesitating, Tobias frowned and pulled out his

sword.

Najal drew a cloth from a pocket in his voluminous black cape and polish the bloodied blade then set the sword across his knees. Lifting his lined face, he chanted, swaying slightly.

Tobias and Sabina exchanged glances. They couldn't understand a word.

Najal stopped abruptly and handed the sword to Tobias.

Tobias gripped the hilt. A force shot through him and he lurched back. A vision of his brother and uncle issuing orders to an army seared his brain, then just as rapidly the image disappeared. Dropping the sword, Tobias staggered up, eyes dilated.

Sabina grabbed his limp hand. "What was it?"

"M—my brother Agaras. I saw him and my uncle."

Najal's dry voice cut the air like a knife. "What else?"

"They were giving orders to a large army of soldiers. An army far greater in size than any in Raveria," Tobias blurted. "I am afraid Theo and Adlar are in trouble. Why else would there be an army preparing for battle, where could they be though."

"Are you sure Tobias?" Sabina said. "We should find your brother Adlar then."

"Yes, I am sure of it. I saw the crown of Raveria too. Larrius had it so I know they are in Tatilan," Tobias said.

"Can you not see where his brother is and

what is going on, Najal?" Sabina asked.

"I wish I could. But like I said before, our power is dwindling and we only use it when we feel most necessary, which is not now. Until we gain more fuel for our power. This is your concern now. Go back home and prevent war," Najal explained. "War is something Fallendor cannot handle again. You two must leave immediately."

Tobias and Sabina frantically stood up and made their way back to the boat. Najal followed them behind as he was slow to keep up.

"We are in danger. I am certain my brother Agaras wants to wage war on all of Fallendor for some reason," Tobias suggested.

"Let's hurry. If they are coming, we have to warn the people of Raveria. And then warn Azden," Sabina admitted.

"Thank you for your help Najal, goodbye," Tobias shouted back to the slow Najal.

"Remember, do not abuse your gift Tobias, use it wisely. The more you use it the more your real self-mind risks being poisoned. Thank you for clearing the way to the other side, now we can explore. Farewell you two," Najal yelled from afar.

Tobias helped Sabina into the boat and they made their way back across the Grey Sea. It was cooler on the water than around the fire on the island. Sabina was rustling around inside the boat and looking for a blanket. She found a small blanket that was slightly damp from the misty rain that had sprinkled a large portion of their time on Rozann. Sabina thought anything to add a little extra warmth would be good enough.

"You cold Sabina?" Tobias asked as he was the one paddling the boat this time. He truly was a quick learner.

"Are you not cold?" Sabina asked.

"Of course not. Besides we will be back in the sunshine soon enough," Tobias replied.

"Where did you go? What was in the cave?" Sabina asked.

Tobias was reluctant to answer. He looked away and slowly kept paddling.

"Uh, Tobias?"

"Oh sorry. It's really nothing, just this jewel," Tobias placed the paddle down and pulled out the shining stone out of his pocket.

"Why did you take that? You fool!" Sabina yelled as she was wide eyed and stunned.

Tobias was completely thrown off by Sabina's aggression.

"When you were still on the mountain I was talking to those creepy men. They said they desired a jewel in the cave but had no way of getting it. A jewel with unknown power they so desperately wanted because it could give them power to get back to their world," Sabina continued.

"For many years that cave was guarded by the beast, so they were unable to get it," Sabina said.

Tobias turned around and glanced off toward

the island of Rozann worried that he may have angered the sorcerers. They had no way of getting off the island anyways he thought, but they did have the power to see into minds, so there was no doubt they would find out eventually. Tobias was worried they already knew he had the jewel.

"I thought they wanted to get through the cave so they could explore the other side of the island?" Tobias asked as he put the jewel away again.

"I know they wanted to explore but they also wanted the jewel. I do not know why. They never said. But let us be thankful they are away from us for a while," Sabina admitted.

Tobias had other things to worry about. He knew he had to warn all of Raveria of a possible invasion from Tatilan. Tobias continued to look out into the sea as he steered their way home. The gentle breeze from the sea felt refreshing on Tobias and Sabina's worn-down faces. They were at peace out on the sea but Proda was now in their sights.

"I do not think my brother Adlar and Theo got to Tatilan in time to stop Agaras," Tobias explained.

"Where are they then?" Sabina asked.

"I am unsure. They could be locked up as prisoners or dead."

"Can you not use your sword and see? Maybe they are back in Mouro."

"It does not work like that. Apparently, you are stuck with the person you are mostly enemies with for good. The power of the sword knows your enemy."

"Could I use it to see? Maybe I can pretend I hate your brother so I can see if they are even alive."

"You heard Najal. I cannot abuse the power. Let's just get off this boat," Tobias said.

Tobias was quick to jump out onto the sandy beach, it felt good to be home he thought. He helped Sabina out of the small boat, and they pulled the boat up onto the shoreline.

"Hey, you brought the boat back," the fisherman said, who was waiting for their return.

"Just as promised," Tobias replied.

"Listen, we need horses now, ours are gone," Sabina asked.

"Yes, and we need to deliver a message. Can we borrow some horses?" Tobias said to the fisherman.

"You two seem trustworthy enough, right this way." The man said leading them behind what seemed to be his house.

"They are not the biggest or fastest horses in Raveria. But they are strong," the man said. The horses looked like they were a little larger than a pony. Anything would have done for Tobias and Sabina who had to hurry back to the city.

"Thank you, sir. We will send someone back with your horses plus gold. Take care," Tobias said. Sabina and Tobias hopped on the small horses and left so fast they could hardly hear if the fisherman said anything back.

"If my brother is in the capital already, we have to warn them," Tobias acclaimed. "I will go straight to Mouro to warn my brother then send someone to deliver a message to the King of Azden."

"What about me?" Sabina asked.

"You need to warn the people of Proda that we need their help. Get Byrim to come. And the rest of the Proda army. You can send someone to Bedria as well to ask for aid, tell them their steward Theo needs them. We will need everyone if this war truly is coming," Tobias explained.

Tobias and Sabina arrived at a point of the road that led to Proda and the other road led toward Mouro. It was getting dark out but there would be enough light out hopefully for the rest of Tobias' ride to the capital city.

"Sabina. This is where we part ways for now. When you have delivered your messages. Return to Mouro and join us. Find the commander and tell him to march out no later than sunrise tomorrow. Thanks again for saving my life. Goodbye friend," Tobias said.

"Farewell Tobias. I hope maybe you can repay the favour on the battlefield one day," Sabina said with a smile. Tobias and Sabina parted ways and continued separately by themselves.

When Tobias arrived in Mouro it was very dark. The night sky had turned as black as the cave was on Rozann. A few stars were starting to poke out which Tobias admired. Tobias got inside the city walls, there was an uneasy silence amongst the city. Only a few guards stood awake. Tobias rushed through the courtyard up to Adlar's room but was surprised not to find him there. He ran back down the steps to the King's Hall, and again, no one was seen. Tobias was worried, what he assumed was turning into reality. Maybe Theo and Adlar were gone forever; he wondered to himself as he paced the city walls frantically. Finally, he asked a guard he ran into.

"You there, where is my brother? Where is King Adlar and Theo?" Tobias questioned.

The guard lifted his shoulders in question. "They are not back yet, no sign of the King's boat in the harbor yet either, I am sorry you were not made aware of this."

Tobias had a look of defeat and disappointment on his face. He rushed into the armory and found a group of men hanging around.

"You men, go to Adon Harbor. Make sure Densis has taken a crew in his ship south to find our king already," Tobias demanded.

The men were quick to oblige.

Tobias saw two more standing about. "You there, send word to the King of Azden immediately," he ordered.

Tobias had now more than ever assumed the worse was about to come. He had seen an army of Tatilan alongside his twin and uncle. Tobias hoped his messages would receive word before it was too late. Tobias went back into the courtyard and sat on the stone bench he often found himself pondering on. Under the calm starry night Tobias sat. Tobias thought to himself that he had so many questions for Najal and the sorcerers still. He grabbed his sword again, he wondered what Najal meant about not using the sword as often but he had to see his brother again. Another jolt of energy rushed through his veins as he grabbed the sword. Tobias could not believe what he saw:

The Tatilan army, led by King Larrius and Agaras had made their way to the shores of the small village Gwen. The army was slaughtering all in their path. Even the women and children were being beaten and killed as everyone in the village quickly diminished. The small village had no chance of fighting off these invaders. Houses were being torched and not a soul that lived there survived. They were helpless. Word of this attack would never have gotten out because of how quick and ruthless the massacre was. King Larrius and his men showed no mercy at all. King Larrius ordered his men to burn the dead bodies and set up camp. They started setting up a little bit away from the village they just depleted. The camp was tucked in the trees at the bottom of a mountain just east of Dal Bantos. They were still several miles away from Dal Bantos, a small city in the south. Larrius started to talk to his new captain, Agaras.

"Agaras, are you excited to take over Fallendor with me?" Larrius asked.

"Of course, uncle. How long until we get back to Raveria?" Agaras said.

"We will take our time getting through Azden. Be patient. Tomorrow we conquer the city of Dal Bantos. And then we will make our way to Endavald," King Larrius said with a twisted smile.

"I am excited," Agaras admitted with a soft smile.

"Get some rest dear boy," Larrius suggested.

Tobias stopped looking and put away his sword. He was disgusted to have just seen a village get massacred at the hands of his brother and uncle. A tear started to creep down Tobias' cold cheek. Tobias couldn't believe what he just witnessed. He knew Dal Bantos, and the rest of Azden was in great danger.

Tobias knew he had to act quickly. He hoped sending a ship to find his other brother and Theo would help, but he needed them right now more than ever. Still, Tobias sat sad and alone and unaware where his brother was. Sending word to the King of Azden was a smart thing to do as well. Tobias knew his men would make it to the eastern country in time. The king lived in Endavald, which is the capital city of Azden. Tobias thought he would not take the news of this attack kindly. Tobias had done all he could for now. He sent a messenger to the King of Azden and had Sabina inform Proda and Bedria of their need for help. Tobias was right to assume the worse when he first saw Agaras with such a large army. He had to prepare his own armies of Raveria to help the rest of Azden. Tobias stood up and thought for a moment that he would bring the soldiers of Mouro to Azden now. He realized it would be a few days for the other armies of Raveria to arrive in the capital. There was no more time to wait, Tobias wanted to lead the Mouro army to aid their eastern neighbors in the morning, and he informed the army to pack their belongings for their march to their eastern neighbors. Tobias meandered alone through the quiet streets of Mouro after he gave word of his plan to lead the army himself, he wondered to himself, *am I too young to lead an army to war?* He found a place to sleep for the night, back at his favorite bench in the courtyard. Most would deem uncomfortable on the firm stoned bench, but not Tobias. He was sad that feeling loneliness had started to become a regular feeling. He gazed at the starry night that twinkled hope into the dark skies and fell fast asleep.

CHAPTER NINE

Adlar and Theo laid wide awake, very still and barely alive. The only thing that could be heard was the sound of waves crashing against the rocks. It had been over a week since they crashed on the island of Demar. They both were dirty and had cuts all over their bodies. They had been living off the meat from the great horned beast that they killed, but all was now gone. Other food was very sparse, if you could even call it food. The two spent time on the island scouring the island and could not find any sustainable food. Adlar and Theo were lucky to be able to keep the fire that Maxall first lit when they arrived on Demar. The boys spent most of their days collecting small, dry branches to keep the flame burning. It was their only source of heat and their only way to cook the small bits of meat, that they had to ration. That flame had become their sole life source, on that wet and chilly piece of rock. Adlar and Theo would explore the island for mainly wood and a hope that maybe they would come across another source of food, but were often left empty handed. The island was filled with unlimited wood from the dense forests, but the boys started to wonder why nothing to be eaten could be found. They were starving and it showed, as their faces were becoming very pale and flush. Theo and Adlar had built a tiny structure out of wood and some remaining supplies that were left behind, one big enough for both of them to squeeze into. This structure also protected the flame from the rain and it seemed to be working. However, with every passing day, and with rain often coming down hard, the two brothers knew it was only a matter of time until their flame went out. The two gathered branches and piled them up by their fire. Supplies left by the men they lost when they first got washed up on Demar were also stacked up to block the wind from putting out the fire. Adlar and Theo were able to build a decent shelter, considering their lack of experience building, so the boys had to be on the lookout for any possible attack. If another beast came, the shelter could easily be destroyed, but so far, this structure had served Adlar and Theo well.

It was Adlar that moved first. A loan moan

erupted from his body as he rolled over and dry heaved. After he was done, he rolled onto his back, holding his injured shoulder.

Adlar and Theo had not done much talking over the last few days. They were still in shock about what had happened. Seeing their crew and Maxall ripped apart by a ferocious wild beast was traumatizing. The lack of water and food was getting to them as well. They had to keep up their strength and it was hard for them at times to even talk. What could they even talk about, they were miserable. The loss of Maxall and the others was weighing on Adlar and Theo greatly. Adlar finally broke the silence.

"Theo, we do not have much time. I can barely move. We have no more food, and no one is coming to find us. We have barely slept because we have had to keep this fire going. What's the point?"

"Adlar, you should get some rest. I will keep the flame going."

"Are you sure? We both need rest."

"I am in better shape than you, I can get up."

Theo rose from the ground and didn't even wince, he couldn't let Adlar see how much it took him to stand.

"Wake me up in a few hours and you can take a turn sleeping. Keep the fire going."

Luckily Adlar didn't argue as he pulled a small piece of clothing over his bruised shoulders and fell fast asleep.

Theo was very tired as well, but he could not

sleep until Adlar woke up. The two boys were both very stubborn and knew they would argue over who would stay awake first. They cared for each other so much even though they had not seen each other for some time. Theo knew he just had to stay awake a little longer. With tired eyes Theo stared into the fire. What are they going to do? A distant light penetrating the darkness pulled him from his thoughts. A light? In the sea? Theo rubbed his eyes. He had to be hallucinating. He focused intently on the light, wishing for it to be real, until his eyes dropped and he fell asleep.

As Adlar and Theo slept, the fire went out, leaving ashes in its wake. In the darkness, eleven men, decked out in black armor, pulled a boat onto the shore.

"Quiet," Manum said.

Peering into the darkness Manum let out a groan. He couldn't see anything. Just then, the moon shifted into position right over the boys. He could just make out the shapes of Adlar and Theo. Manum chuckled. This was going to be too easy.

"Alright men, you know what to do," Manum whispered. "Kill the oldest brother and capture the other man as our prisoner."

"What is that approaching?" an assassin said.

"It looks like a large boat or something," another man said.

"Quick, run to the bushes," Manum demanded.

The assassins ran into the forest unaware what was coming toward the island. A few moments passed and a ship appeared from the shadow of the night. It was Maxall's brother. As well as several soldiers. They were in the ship that Theo and Adlar were first supposed to take to Tatilan. It was fixed and they were here to rescue King Adlar and Theo.

Manum and his men felt trapped because they assumed this ship was coming from Raveria and were outnumbered.

"You two, quietly go back in the boat and let my father know we couldn't kill the king, but we will," Manum explained.

"What about the rest of you? We can just wait for them and kill them all," a man asked.

"We are going to Raveria. Come men we are sneaking on the ship when everyone clears out," Manum said.

The two assassins left in the boat and paddled back to Tatilan.

"What if they see us?" A man said with a high-pitched voice.

"You are right. Dump our armor here. Leave the weapons as well," Manum suggested.

"If anyone sees us on board, we will say we came from Raveria, no one will question us if were unarmed," Manum continued.

It was hard to distinguish the difference between those from Tatilan or Raveria anyways. Except for Manum's noticeably dark eyes and scar on the side of his face that came down from his eyebrow. He looked like he had never been happy, just like his father Larrius, so it would be relatively easy to play as Raverian men Manum assumed.

"Come on!" Manum said as the group quietly strolled through the dense forest toward the ship.

"Wait for the last man to leave the ship. Then we will board," Manum continued.

The ship stopped just along the cliffs, and was nestled right up against the rock.

The last crew member left the ship and Manum ordered his men to quietly sneak on board which they did without being spotted.

Those who were on the ship had all left to assist Theo and Adlar now that they located them.

The two boys were surprised to be woken up by people.

"What is going on?" Theo said in a daze.

"We came to rescue you. I sensed you were in danger," said a man.

"I am Maxall's brother Densis. Where is he now?"

"He is gone," Adlar explained. "Your brother died trying to save us."

Densis choked up by the news, holding his hands to his face. Theo and Adlar wanted more than ever to leave the island which was apparent when they quickly got up and gathered what they had left. Adlar and Theo were not in the mood for consoling Densis right now, they just wanted to get off this rock. They packed their belongings they had left and headed toward the ship.

"Come. We will talk on the ship," Theo suggested.

Everyone sulked on their way to the ship. Densis was still in tears weeping at the news of his older brother's death. All were aboard the ship and they made their way back out into the Grey Sea.

Densis was at the wheel, quietly steering. He had similar curly hair to Maxall but it was much lighter.

Adlar and Theo came up to the captain's deck to see Densis.

"We appreciate you coming for us Densis," Adlar said.

"How did you know we were here?" Theo asked.

Densis whipped away a tear before he replied.

"We saw a little boat at the side there as we were sailing by. Figured it was you two," Densis exclaimed.

"We had a boat but it sank. Why do you think we were still here? You didn't see a boat," Adlar mentioned.

"I could have sworn I saw a boat. It's gone now so it doesn't matter. We found you," Densis stated calmly.

"So, about my brother. What happened?" Densis asked.

"We were attacked by a beast. It killed

everyone but us, we are the only survivors," Adlar said as he almost choked up. There was silence between everyone again.

"I knew you brother very well. It's sad to see him go," Adlar said, who had his arm around Densis.

"He will be missed. If only he could see his finished ship out at sea," Densis said quietly.

"You have done your brother proud Densis. The ship looks truly wonderful," Theo said excitedly.

Adlar and Theo looked at each other and finally felt at peace. They weren't always the only two on the island. They were happy to know that no other beast had come for them while they struggled to survive. Alas though they were saved.

"Alright, onward to Raveria," shouted Densis, who now had the ship turned around.

"Guys, grab some food. You look terrible," Densis said to Adlar and Theo.

Densis had the massive wooden ship on course back to Raveria. It had taken them much less time to get this far down south. The ship was quick blasting through the waters of the sea. It would be morning by the time they arrived home.

Morning did come fast as the ship had arrived at Adon Harbor. The sun was shining in Raveria and the people in the harbor village were anxiously awaiting the arrival of the king. Densis anchored the ship and everyone hopped out onto a wooden dock that had beams coming from the side to make it possible for the crew to exit the ship.

"Leave it for the dockmaster. He will take care of the ship. Let's go," Densis said as he and Adlar were the last one's off.

Adlar was thanking Densis for rescuing them, when he looked up and spotted Livia from beyond the dock. He raced off to see her. Adlar instantly smiled and ran toward her in the harbor. Livia was smiling back at Adlar as she leaped into his arms. The people were welcoming everyone else as well and the village became very crowded with the ships welcoming.

"It is so good to see you my Livia," Adlar said as he gave a kiss.

"I missed you. I thought of you every day. I did not know if I would ever see you again," Adlar said, continuing to stare at Livia as if he didn't think she was real.

"I missed you too Adlar," Livia said with a smile. "Today is the first day in a while we have had sunshine. So, I always knew today was going to be a grand day."

"I do not want to lose you again dear sweet Livia. I want you to be my queen. I think I am in love with you. My love for you has grown so strong since I met you. I thought of this while I was away. I want to marry you. Will you take my hand and be my wife and my queen?" Adlar asked.

He knew it was what his heart wanted. Livia was shocked. Her brown eyes lit up. Her eyes watered ever so slightly, as if she was moments from tears, but

she took a deep breath, smiled at King Adlar.
"Yes!" Livia replied ecstatically.
Livia and Adlar kissed again in the busy crowds of the markets.
"Let's go to Mouro. We should inform the country of our engagement," Adlar suggested.
The two were overjoyed and couldn't stop smiling. Adlar and Livia held hands and walked toward the capital. Theo was ahead of them patiently waiting for them with some horses to ride to the city. Adlar and Theo were anxious to get back and see Tobias. The news of the engagement, as well as the safe arrival home would be well received by the people of Mouro.

A wedding was still to be planned, and a lot of work was to be done, but in the customs of tradition, a wedding for the king was usually prepared quickly.

At the ship, the dockmaster was making his final inspections. He noticed a few men rustling on the ship.
"Eh, you men, get off the ship, I see you there, no time for doodling. Let's go," the dockmaster stammered to the men.
"Yes, right away sir, we just woke up," a man said.
The dockmaster had a confused look on his face. He thought everyone had already left the ship. Nothing seemed out of the ordinary for these men looked like ones that accompanied the others. It was

Manum and his group that no one on board ever suspected otherwise.

"We came to aid the retrieval of the king," Manum said as he appeared from behind a beam.

"We are from the north; we were told by the king to come on their journey south. But now we have no place to stay, the north is a long journey for us. Can we stay at an inn here until we are ready to leave?" Manum asked with a rare charming demeanor.

The dockmaster had no idea what else to say other than welcome them to the harbor.

"Of course, any friend of the king is a friend of mine right this way," the dockmaster said as he led Manum and his men through the crowds to a local inn just past the markets in the village.

"I think this place on the right will do you men well," the dockmaster kindly said. "Tell them I sent you folk and they'll set you up nicely."

"Much appreciated kind sir," Manum replied.

Manum and his eight men had successfully made their way to Raveria. They planned on staying for as long as they had to before their job to slay the king was finished. Manum knew that this was unfamiliar territory and time wasn't on their side because sooner or later someone would find out who they really are.

CHAPTER TEN

Adlar, Theo and Livia and the rest of the crew received a warm welcome. Adlar was happy to be back in his beloved city. Through the crowds and the loud roars from the people of Mouro, Adlar was surprised not to see Tobias. Cheers echoed off the stone walls of the capital but they didn't faze the king. Adlar had a look of confusion on his sallow face and he quickly helped Livia off his horse. They forced a path through the people and made their way to Adlar's chambers to look for Tobias.

"Where are we going?" asked Livia, trying her best to keep up with Adlar.

"My brother Tobias should be here, but is not," he explained.

"Where could he be Adlar?" Theo asked.

That is why we are heading to my chamber, where else could he be? Adlar thought.

The three hastened up the stone steps toward the king's room. Guards welcomed them as they passed. As they entered the room, Tobias was nowhere to be found. Adlar kicked over his wooden stool.

Livia was shocked to see him this angry; she had only seen Adlar as a sweet genuine king. "Maybe he went to his own home?" Livia said softly.

"I told him to stay here. He would be mindless to leave," Adlar said.

"He is still just a young boy who has not quite grown into a man," Theo replied.

"Come on let us see if a guard knows where he is," Adlar said.

They left the room and quickly found a guard.

"Where is Tobias?" Theo asked him.

"Your brother left. With your army. They're going to Azden," the guard replied.

Theo and Adlar glanced at each other in shock. They ambled back to the courtyard hoping this was all a dream and that Tobias would finally be waiting for them there like the rest of the capital.

When they arrived, the streets had already emptied. Just a few stranglers remaining, most having returned to the markets. Adlar called out for a guard, but there was no response. As he looked around, frustrated, a young girl poked her head around a small bush, pausing as she picked a handful of bright pink begonias. She stared at Livia as if she'd never seen a human before.

"Your brother Tobias is at war," she said quietly. "My father left with him and the army. I miss my daddy already."

The thought of war scared Adlar, and he was worried for the safety of his brother and country.

"At war? With whom?" he asked.

"I do not know, I am only ten," the girl said as she dropped the bouquet of flowers and ran away.

"King Adlar, your brother Tobias must know something we do not. Maybe he is at war with Azden. But why," Theo exclaimed.

"Or against them, we have to leave right away," Adlar said. "We need to leave immediately."

Adlar gathered up the begonias and handed them to Livia.

"My sweet Livia, we will arrange for our wedding when I return. But I have to go. See to it that the servant girls take good care of you," Adlar suggested patiently.

"No, do not leave me. I have already lost you once, I do not want it to happen again," Livia said with sadness in her soft voice.

"I must go, I will always be with you, my lady," King Adlar said as he kissed Livia.

"Goodbye Adlar, stay safe," Livia said while she smelt her freshly picked flowers.

The brothers rushed away and out of the courtyard.

"Let's go Adlar, we can get to Azden by nightfall tomorrow if we hurry," Theo said eagerly.

Adlar and Theo left and gathered some things they thought they would need, then headed back down to the stables. Adlar wished he could have his crown, but he did pack his newly crafted helmet, forged from Raverian steel. He would certainly need all the armor he could get if battle awaits. Adlar thought nothing could be more special and honorable than wearing his crown and had hoped to retrieve it soon, he didn't feel like a king without it. Himself and Theo both hopped on their horses quickly and raced down the dusty path leading from the front gate of the city walls. They had no time to waste, for the other armies of the North had already made their way to Azden, but they would need all the help they could get.

Leading the Raverian army, Tobias was alone at the front line, unaware of what he was about to face. His men crossed King's Bridge, which separates the borders of Raveria and Azden. Tobias peered off the road and let his general lead the troops forward in perfect sync. He kept watch but quickly grabbed his sword, hoping to not make too much of a scene, Tobias jarred back a bit, nearly falling off his horse and his vision dive into the mind of his twin brother Agaras.

Smoke and wreckage were all that was left of

the city of Dal Bantos. King Larrius and his Tatilanian army made waste of the southern part of Azden. With no real military threat in the south and being outnumbered, Tatilan men were able to slaughter all in the city. They made prisoners of the women and children. This beautiful city had been lost. Endavald was now all that separated King Larrius and his men from Raveria. Larrius saw through Adlar's crown that small help from Adlar and Theo and few men was on their way from the north. That didn't stop the King from Tatilan from slaughtering all in his army's way. Larrius decided to build up their defenses and wait for an attack from the north, rather than march onward. Agaras believed the same as the two stood side by side watching part of Dal Bantos burn.

"You saw my brother, King Adlar coming to Azden?" Agaras asked.

"I did. We do not need to see any more, put this crown away," Larrius said, handing over the crown of Raveria over.

"We will stay put here. This will give us an advantage by resting and gathering our strength for any approaching army from the north," King Larrius continued.

"I agree it will be much easier to decimate their armies by waiting for them here," Agaras said.

King Larrius was the man he had been rumored to be, wicked and ruthless. He was a patient man though and if it meant waiting weeks for an attack from Azden then he would wait. "Get some sleep boy. But keep that crown handy. I will need it sometime soon I reckon. And if I catch you spying on your brother with it without my permission you will regret it," King Larrius said as Agaras obliged and left his uncles tent.

    Tobias sheathed his sword and returned to the frontline. He ordered a few men to march ahead alongside him to Endavald, the capital city of Azden. The rest of his soldiers were now setting up camp while they waited for a signal before rejoining them. The men were tucked just beside the forest before the city of Endavald. Azden was known for its beautiful and luscious forests. Tall thick trees that could be seen from miles away. Tobias and a few men trotted along lush grasslands toward the city. Tobias wondered what kind of reaction he would get from the king. Although he had never met him before; he had only heard about him. Yet, Tobias had never even been this far east, so he had no idea what to expect from the people of Azden either. As Tobias and his men got closer to the city walls, they started to realize soldiers marching out of the gate. They rushed quickly to the entrance to see where the soldiers were going. Tobias was in amazement as he approached that he had to stop and admire the colossal size and beauty of Endavald. The city walls were built from a strong stone that was only found in these parts. The very thought of anyone destroying such beauty didn't sit well with Tobias. He was left speechless from the sight of the city walls. Tobias needed to find the King so he didn't have time for admiring castle walls.

"Halt!" an Endavald guard yelled.

"Do not go any further," the guard continued as everyone's attention now seemed to be on Tobias.

"I am from Raveria. I must speak to your King, I have an urgent message, your city is in danger," Tobias quickly replied.

"Oh, we know, it is just some foreign scum from the south, we will destroy them quickly, go back to where you came from," another guard said.

"You do not understand, I saw the army coming this way. They have double, maybe even triple the men you have here," Tobias said.

"Are you deaf, boy? Beat it, no army can match ours, even if they do have a bigger army, we will defeat anyone, you are mad to think otherwise," the guard once again replied.

"What seems to be the situation here General Rius?" A voice appeared from behind the group of gathered troops.

"This foreign rat from the north wants to speak to you my lord," Rius explained.

The man appeared out of the crowd. Based on the sudden ease around the crowds Tobias thought this was the king of Azden. He was tall and thin; he had a skinny nose and pointy jaw. His blue eyes were bright as a summer sky.

"Can I help you?" the tall man said.

"Are you the King?" Tobias asked. "I have come to warn you. My name is Tobias, brother of the King of Raveria. I have seen the army from the south that are here in Azden, we are all in danger. My uncle Larrius has already made waste of Dal Bantos and Endavald is next," Tobias frantically continued without allowing the man to speak.

"I am the king you seek. King Aegnor of Azden," Aegnor said calmly. "How do you know of this attack from the south if you are coming from the north boy?"

"We do not have any time," Tobias said, still getting lost in the beauty of the city. He was still only at the entrance way he thought of how wonderful inside must look.

"Tobias, I admire your bravery to come all this way to warn us, but go home, we don't need northerners help, we will fight and we will destroy the invaders that come this way, I am sending men right now to launch our defense of this great nation," Aegnor said with confidence and belief in his army.

"I brought an army with me to help you, just believe me when I say this army from the south is bigger than you can imagine, you need our help," Tobias said desperately.

"General Rius, stall the march and wait for my command," King Aegnor said as General Rius obeyed.

"If this is some kind of joke you are dead," Aegnor said as he gave Tobias an unnerving look.

A scream then a yell came out from the crowd of soldiers. "King Aegnor, come quick!" a soldier shouted.

The king, along with Tobias rushed toward the commotion. Laying on the ground was a battered and bloodied woman.

"What happened?" King Aegnor asked. There was a long silence before the woman gathered the strength to speak.

"Invaders, they came and they slaughtered everyone. My husband, my children," the woman said in distraught.

"There is hardly anything left standing in Dal Bantos, they spared some of the women and children. For their own pleasures of course, but I was able to escape the madness. I came to warn you, their army is large, very large. We do not stand a chance," the woman said with tears slowly rolling down her cheek.

"Thank you for warning us, and I am sorry about your family, we will avenge your family. Go into the city and my servants will take care of you," Aegnor said as the lady was helped to her feet.

"You see, I wasn't making this up," Tobias was quick to say.

"This is now the second person in two days that has come from Dal Bantos in distress to warn us." He turned toward Tobias. "Can you help us?" King Aegnor asked as he pulled out a piece of parchment.

King Aegnor placed the parchment paper on a small wooden table that was just out front the gate. It had landmarks of the country on it.

"Is this supposed to be Azden?" Tobias asked.

"No time for messing about, of course it is Azden," Aegnor rebuked.

Tobias gave an odd and confusing look. He thought his question wasn't as dumb as the King made it sound. Fallendor wasn't a place that really had a map. Only very rough major landmarks tell people of certain places. Never has a detailed map even been created.

"Well, I am no expert. But I suggest we send in your army full on. And I will send my army into these forests here and wait until we can ambush them from behind," Tobias said.

"They will be expecting only your army, so I hope our element of surprise will benefit us."

"Hmmm, very interesting," Aegnor said as he rubbed his chiseled chin in deep thought.

"What do you think, general?" Aegnor asked.

"The young boy from the north seems wise. I would have thought this same approach," Rius agreed confidently.

"I will take my army through this forest here to the left and stay there. When you have engaged in battle with the enemy, we will ambush them from behind," Tobias gave his idea to an impressed Aegnor.

"What if this does not work?" Aegnor asked.

"It may not work. But we have to fight together and hope that we can protect Fallendor,"

Tobias admitted.

"But, when shall we move out? My men are ready now," Aegnor asked.

"Nightfall is upon us," Rius said. "I reckon we should leave now."

"My brother and the steward of Bedria might be here by this time tomorrow, but we should not wait much longer," Tobias said. "I sent word to the cities of Raveria to aid us. They too may arrive by morning."

"Let us wait until morning then, if we can wait for reinforcements that will help us greatly," King Aegnor acclaimed.

"Armies from Proda, as well as from Bedria should be here by morning," Tobias said. "I sure hope."

"We will wait until sunrise to attack; we will wait for help from the other northern armies," King Aegnor agreed.

"I hope this works. I will go inform my men of our plan now, I will be back," Tobias said. He walked away slowly back to his horse where it had remained with his guards. Tobias felt Aegnor watching his every step, so Tobias turned around to lock eyes with the king.

"Tobias, how have you seen the army from the south if you say you are from the north," King Aegnor asked.

Tobias' eyes widened in fear, he did not know how he could answer this. His face whitened as

Aegnor waited for Tobias to speak.
"I thought I dreamt about it, I suppose," Tobias replied.

"You are lying to me," Aegnor replied firmly as he got closer to Tobias.

"I would not lie to you; how else could I know?" Tobias quickly said back.

"Tell me the truth," Aegnor was persistent to get an honest answer.

"I do speak the truth. I have had dreams like this before that have come real. My father told me never to ignore these dreams," Tobias explained.

"Well fine, go on and get your men ready then and get some rest as well dear boy. Tomorrow we will see one another again," Aegnor said as he returned inside the city.

Tobias was lost wandering in his mind if it was right to lie to King Aegnor of his secret. It would certainly help them win this battle. However, Tobias thought the King would use it against him or desire it from himself. He thought he would use the sword when he returned to the Raverian camp, just to see where Agaras was. Darkness was settling in so he figured he would wait until morning to see. Tobias and his guards arrived back at the forest the rest of the army had been making camp.

"Men, we are going to battle tomorrow, spread the word to others. We attack at sunrise, get some rest you will all need it," Tobias said, who now turned to general Cirdan. "General, any word from

Sabina? Any word from armies from Proda or Bedria? I fear they will not be here by tomorrow morning."

"I have not seen any sign of anyone. I have a guard on watch for their arrival at King's Bridge," Cirdan explained firmly.

"Very well, I am going to try and get some sleep," Tobias said as he gathered up some blankets and laid down.

Tobias never could sleep well; he knew he would be up tossing and turning all night. Anxiously and nervously imagining what this upcoming battle would be like. His main worry now was where Sabina and the other armies of Raveria were. Tobias also wondered if Adlar and Theo were alive and coming to their aid. He would wonder all night about if they would even be here by morning to help the attack.

CHAPTER ELEVEN

Horns sounded and morning had come quickly. It was still the beginning of the first month of summer. A thick fog had cast across the lands of Azden. This beautiful country had lost its southern city. For the sake of all of Fallendor, Endavald couldn't be allowed to fall either. Being overrun was not an option for anyone who stood in the way of the great threat of Tatilan. These horns belonged to Proda and Bedria; the armies from the north had finally arrived. A couple thousand soldiers, fully armored, marched across King's Bridge and into Endavald. The front line was led by Sabina and Byrim. They were greeted by Tobias who had rushed out from his slumber to greet them.

"You made it," Tobias said with a giant grin

on his face.

"Aw, did you miss me?" Sabina joked back. She was never one for romance, which she had made clear. They had grown very close having become great friends since their venture to Rozann.

"Good to see you as well Byrim," Tobias said.

"Let's go to the city, the King Aegnor awaits us. We will attack soon," Tobias said as he hopped on his horse and darted across the grass, which was damp from the morning dew.

The tall trees casted shadows, that contributed to the dimness. Even though it was still morning, the sun had not quite settled above the lands that were soon to become a battleground.

"Byrim, inform General Cirdan that we are marching to Endavald. Sabina and I are going ahead," Tobias explained.

"Of course, Tobias," Byrim replied.

Tobias and Sabina arrived at the front gate, where Azden troops prepared for battle. A golden ray of sunlight pierced through some trees and shined on the army. King Aegnor was giving his final instructions to his men when he saw Tobias and Sabina arrive.

"Tobias, I hear our reinforcements have arrived. Are they ready?" King Aegnor asked.

"Of course, our soldiers have been training many years for a fight. We will march to the forest right away and await our signal to ambush," Tobias said.

"Very well then, I hope to see you back here again young man, farewell and good luck," Aegnor said as he began heading off to prepare his men for battle.

"You are not coming?" Tobias asked in shock.

"I am the king; I do not have time for war. My generals will lead the way for all of Azden. Take care."

Tobias and Sabina noticed some Raverian soldiers already approaching from behind. The two of them hustled to join the soldiers. The combined forces of the three cities of the north made up nearly four thousand soldiers. These numbers didn't exactly add up to those of Tatilan but would certainly help defending against the foreign invaders attack. Tobias had seen the strength and size of the Tatilan army, and knew his forces would need some sort of a miracle if they were to have a chance.

Tobias gave his orders and alongside Sabina led the soldiers to the forest. It would be hard to be seen by the enemy in the dark shadow that hid the army among the trees and dense brush. Raverian soldiers were protected by shining silver armor. Raveria was known for its fine blacksmiths and for the mining of the rare and fine material used to craft such strong armor. Strong armor was what their men needed, whose strength was engaging in hand to hand combat, needed. The soldiers arrived in the forest and out of sight of their enemy. Tobias signal led Sabina to follow him as they got away from the army and hid behind some bushes. Tobias explained to Sabina that he had to use his sword to see Agaras' whereabouts.

"Sabina, keep watch. We cannot let anyone know what I am doing, if word got out it could be our undoing," Tobias said as he grabbed his sword, felt force in his palms and instantly was in the mind of his brother Agaras.

Preparation was occurring north of Dal Bantos. The army from Tatilan was nearly double the size of the combined forces of Raveria and Azden. If numbers won a battle, then victory would be easy for King Larrius and his army.

King Larrius stood calmly with Agaras by his side, his posture undeniably regal. They were suited in black iron armor from the mountains back in Tatilan. From the shouting, it appeared that Agaras and King Larrius were having an argument as morning started to break.

"My king, must I put on the crown for a small moment and see Tobias's whereabouts?" Agaras asked.

King Larrius shook his head. "No! It must not be worn; I need it so I can see when your eldest brother Adlar arrives. He is much more dangerous. If Tobias is anything like what you have told me, he is probably sitting pretty relaxing back in the sunshine of his hometown with a servant girl." He was reluctant to even make eye contact while he spoke to Agaras.

"But, would it not be wise to just see for a second?"

King Larrius seemed infuriated with Agaras and his questions. Larrius stood up and grabbed a hold of Agaras' neck. "Do not ask me again, or this will be the last time you breathe," Larrius firmly said. Agaras' eyes widened in shock, and Larrius' dark eyes bore deep into them. "Of course, my lord," he whispered.

"Alright boy, well let's prepare our troops to attack. I am tired of waiting. And it does not seem like your brother is close to arriving." King Larrius grabbed his sword and walked toward his men as Agaras followed slowly with his head hung low.

Tobias put away his sword. "Sabina, my uncle will not let Agaras use the crown to see where we are. This is massive! Now they really do not know where we are!"

"But when are they attacking? That is the important question," Sabina asked as the two joined the other soldiers.

"I think they are going to be heading to battle now," Tobias responded.

A loud drum echoed from tree to tree, reverberating through the soil on the ground. The Raverian soldiers looked around at each other, silenced by the sudden noises. The sounds were foreign to their ears and seemed to transform as it traveled through the brush.

It was the army from the south. The Tatilan army cheered and roared as they arrived at a large clearing. They were clad in their dark armor led by King Larrius.

Tobias could see through the forest that this army would be very hard to defeat. Thousands of soldiers waited patiently for an attack. Tobias knew that he and his army had to stay quiet and remain unseen. They were nearly twenty meters away from the enemy, so any sort of movement in haste would be easily heard. Tobias hoped to himself that the dense trunks of the tall trees as well as the thick bushes could hide them for at least a little while.

The horns of Azden blared. They had arrived at the plains and stood face to face with their enemy. The Tatilan army outnumbered Azden troops four to one, but those odds were hoping to be improved once the soldiers from Raveria emerged from the forest.

The Azden soldiers were surprised to see the army from the south this close to the city of Endavald. King Larrius had hoped to take the battle a little further away from the city, but now had no choice but to put in a good fight.

The plains of Azden were flourishing as always. A strong breeze from the east trembled the long grass. Leading the Azden army was General Rius. Rius was a trained fighter and very skilled with a sword. The early morning glow of the sun cast a warm, spectacular glow over the field. It was no wonder this country was known for its natural beauty.

Such a pity these lands were about to be turned into rivers of blood and death.

The Tatilan army sent in a few hundred troops on horseback. Azden was greatly known for its long-range archery and General Rius ordered for a cloud of arrows to be sent through the sky.

"Release!" Rius ordered.

Hundreds of arrows were fired toward the cavalry, many connecting with soldiers. The Tatilan horse fleet was decimated by arrows quickly. Nearly half the horsemen sent in were killed. Azden archers sent another lob of arrows and finished off the remaining men.

King Larrius seemed surprised at the range of the Azden arches. Surely, he had heard the stories about the General but had never seen such strong bows.

King Larrius looked infuriated with how easily his horsemen were defeated, they had no chance if they kept sending in small groups of soldiers.

"Agaras, it is time to lead the charge with everyone else," King Larrius demanded.

Agaras followed command with the rest of the men—most of which were on horseback as well. The size of this brigade would not be so easily matched by the Azden arrows. Tatilan was known for its horsemen, which is why their cavalry was in the thousands. Although half of their horses were defeated already.

Agaras led a charge into the Azden defenses, followed behind by the King himself and the remaining men on foot. The archers of Azden weren't as successful with this barrage. The numbers were too great to stop them. Although many arrows took down Tatilan soldiers, the Azden forces were met with sheer anger and rage as the Tatilan army finally penetrated the defenses.

The golden grass, now stained with blood, continued to sway in the breeze—a constant reminder that lives were lost here. Azden's front line of spear men was quickly breached, as Azden soldiers dropped rapidly.

General Rius was spotted, heavily outnumbered by Tatilan soldiers. He swung his sword with fiery accuracy as he tried to fend off as many as he could handle. Rius ended up taking not only an arrow to the neck but a spear to the back.

It was a bloodbath ever since the remaining forces of Tatilan joined the fight. Although Azden soldiers were hanging on and fighting with might and courage, they were being overrun. Tobias could see that their numbers were diminishing quickly so finally took his army into battle.

Tobias lifted his hand. "Come on Sabina. Come on men, it is time for battle," he said, leading the Raverian army alongside Sabina.

"See you after victory my friend," Sabina said with a smile.

Raverian soldiers poured out of the dark

forests and stormed in on the Tatilan forces. The Raverian army arrived at the blood spill of chaos. Tatilan troops were left confused at the sight of reinforcements. They were totally caught off guard as Raverian men crashed through the backline.

It appeared that the element of surprise stunned King Larrius and his men. The Tatilan army was now dropping quickly in numbers. Tobias was fast to spot his uncle and he locked eyes with King Larrius, who appeared not to recognize the young nephew of his. Tobias made a charge for the King right away.

Surrounded by violence, death and chaos, Larrius and Tobias started to duel as they had swords drawn.

"You do not want to do this boy," King Larrius shouted as blood dripped from his pointed chin.

"I do!" Tobias yelled with courage as he attacked King Larrius.

They attacked each other at the same time. King Larrius had been fighting for quite some time already, and he appeared much more tired, and it showed in how difficult it was for him to lift his sword. Tobias dominated the fight using his bravery and a little bit of anger.

Tobias and his uncle's duel waged on for a couple minutes. Tobias had not seen any battle with a sword, so was majorly inexperienced but knew he had to do anything he could to defeat his fading uncle.

Tobias felt a blow to the back of his head which knocked him down into the muddy and bloody ground. A Tatilan soldier had hit Tobias, and now King Larrius stood over top of him.

He placed the tip of his sword onto Tobias' chest. Tobias used all his strength to roll over and get up, just dodging the blade. Tobias clutched a broken end of a spear off a fallen soldier adjacent to him. He quickly turned around and stabbed King Larrius in the neck.

Blood instantly spewed out from the king's neck and gushed out on Tobias' face. There was a quiet halt in the battle as everyone had seen the King of Tatilan drop to his knees and clutching his gushing wound. Azden and Raverian soldiers did not want to stop fighting, so took their chance in trying to catch the Tatilan troops off guard as they watched their king fall in horror. Tatilan soldiers now had no choice but to retreat.

"Retreat! Return to the boats!" Agaras shouted as the Tatilan forces retreated as quickly as possible.

Agaras looked across the battlefield and made eye contact with Tobias. Hazel eyes met hazel eyes, covered in blood and dirt. Agaras turned on his heel and gave Tobias a crooked grin.

Cheers came from all the remaining Azden and Raverian soldiers. They had won, and Tobias stood over his dead uncle's body, looked out into the fields and watched Agaras running away with the enemy. There were still a large number of Tatilan soldiers left. But without their king they had no choice but to retreat, and Tobias watched as they ran back into the surrounding forest.

Tobias bent down and grasped his brother's crown, the crown of Raveria will finally be back in the capital. Tobias' father wore this crown for many years. Touching it—feeling it—the meaning of the crown warmed Tobias, and he let the feeling resonate inside him. Getting it back meant everything. He lifted the crown into the clear skies, and the armies of Raveria and Azden chanted Tobias' name. Tobias stood quietly, he thought about his brother Adlar and why they hadn't come. He then realized that he had not seen Sabina during the whole fight, but figured she was by his side the whole time.

"Sabina, where are you?" Tobias yelled out but got no response.

"Has anyone seen Sabina?" he asked again, frantically looking around.

"She is gone, she lays right there," Byrim said, as he emerged from the soldiers.

Byrim pointed to a body that laid amongst the rest of the fallen. Tobias ran to the body to see if it was Sabina. Tobias fell to his knees to see Sabina motionless, breathless, with a sword in her chest. In an instant, Tobias' pride was shattered, and he was instantly devastated. He threw the crown to the ground and cried as he held onto Sabina's cold and bloodied body.

Weeping, Tobias had no idea what to do while

he held his dear friend's body. Byrim came over to console Tobias.

"Tobias, I am so sorry," Byrim said. "I know how close you two have gotten."

Tobias had tears falling onto Sabina's battered face as he leant over her.

"She would not stop talking about you the whole way we marched to Azden," Byrim said calmly.

"She will be missed greatly," Tobias quietly said motionless.

"Help the wounded and clean up this mess," Byrim yelled back to the soldiers.

Tobias laid Sabina down gently and eyed the crown he had tossed to the soil. "Send everyone back to Endavald, King Aegnor will be awaiting us. He should know of our victory," Tobias said with sadness in his voice.

Tobias stayed with Sabina quietly and sad as evening approached. He had stayed with Sabina a few hours after the final soldier left the battlefield. Tobias wanted to bury Sabina, so he used his helmet and dug her grave.

He wanted to leave her in the plains of Azden, living on in memory where all of Fallendor was saved. The sun was close to setting so Tobias picked himself up and said goodbye. His tears drenched the ground. It was a victorious day for Raveria and Azden, but the loss of Tobias' good friend would be something he would dread for a long time.

CHAPTER TWELVE

The war was over; Tatilan had been defeated. There was no king in the south, and King Larrius' plan had failed. Raverian and Azden troops celebrated their victory inside the palace walls of Endavald. Many lives had been lost, but the lives that the victory saved were well worth it, even for Tobias, who had lost his dear friend Sabina. Tobias still had a look of despair on his pale rugged face as he entered the city. The people in the city chanted his name, making Tobias feel as if he were the real hero of the battle.

    He may as well have been the hero. He killed King Larrius and retrieved the crown of Raveria. Tobias was certainly humbled by the reception he got. King Aegnor had now stepped down from the stairwell that led from the hall and into the opening where people had gathered. Aegnor greeted Tobias with a giant hug. It appeared hard for Tobias to show any joy, as he was still saddened by the loss of Sabina.

"My boy, you are a hero!" King Aegnor said. Tobias gave a delicate smile to show some respect to the King's kind words.

"Cheer up boy, you have guests here to see you," Aegnor said as he pointed off to the crowd. It was Adlar and Theo who were running toward Tobias with open arms.

"Brother, it is so good to see you!" Adlar said as he leaped into Tobias' arms.

"It's been far too long," Tobias replied, overjoyed with the sight of Adlar and Theo.

"Tobias, I am happy to see you alive, did you defeat your brother Agaras for me?" Theo asked.

"He ran off with the rest of the enemy. But our uncle is dead," Tobias admitted.

"Everyone is talking about you Tobias; you are a hero. Father would be very proud of you," Adlar said ecstatically.

Hearing those words made Tobias emotional as he fought back tears. All he ever wanted was to make his father proud of him one day. Tobias looked up to his father like any son would. The fact that he was not around to be with him for this momentous day made him sad.

Tobias wiped a tear that crept out and trickled down his cheek. King Aegnor joined the trio at the front of the courtyard.

"Brothers, let us all gather in the King's hall and discuss where we shall go after our victory," King Aegnor said before addressing the people of Endavald.

"People of Endavald, I ask you to please clear out, there will be time to celebrate, let our hero's rest. Then we can rejoice in this mighty victory together," Aegnor said as he and the two brothers, as well as Theo walked away up the steps to the hall.

Through large stoned doors, the four men entered the King's Hall and were greeted by a small gathering.

All of King Aegnor's council were inside the hall seated at their places. The Queen and daughter were in their throne at the front of the great hall.

"Welcome to the great hall of Endavald. These people here are members of my council, they do not need any proper introduction," King Aegnor announced to the boys before sitting himself down in his throne.

"Now, these two however are my lovely queen, Elena, and my daughter, Enna. They welcome you to the capital."

"Greetings everyone, and thank you for welcoming us in. I am the King of Raveria, and my brother Tobias here is the steward of Proda and this here is Theo, steward of the north," Adlar spoke to the people, wearing his own crown for the first time.

"Brothers of Raveria, we know you have

always been allies of ours. We have always remained to ourselves but in peace. I open the proposition that we aim to work together more and become cohesive in our efforts to keep Azden and Raveria even more safe. Especially from our new stubborn enemies in the south. Together we can unite our nations and work as one to build a strong foundation to protect us from the south. As we found out we are capable of sustaining any threat from the south if we work together as one. We will only get stronger if we can continue this way," Aegnor shouted for all to listen. "Now, I ask
you all, will you unite our nations and become unified alleys?"

Adlar didn't hesitate as he stepped to the front of the hall and said "On behalf of all of us, we agree that this is better for all of us." King Aegnor smiled at the news of this agreement. "Excellent news. Now, one last thing. To unite this bond, I suggest we marry my daughter Enna, with Tobias. The hero of our great victory. This marriage will keep us loyal and united nations. Tobias dear boy, how does this idea sound?" Aegnor faced Tobias who looked surprised by his request.

Tobias was obviously caught off guard. He gawked at his brother. His bravery and courage during the battle earned the respect of King Aegnor. He looked to the throne where Enna sat quietly. She had the look of a warm summer day blanketed on her face, a natural beauty with long blonde hair and a dazzling sparkle in her eyes. At first glance Tobias thought she looked sweet and caring, but he thought for a moment he could not be forced to love someone. In fact, he had no idea what love truly was or marriage for that matter. However, for the sake of Fallendor, Tobias knew this was something he would have to do.

"I will marry your daughter Enna and unite our great nations," Tobias said as all who remained in the great hall rose to their feet. Everyone clapped and rejoiced at the news.

"Wonderful, wonderful. My daughter will be thrilled. We will marry you two as soon as possible. I recommend we make it happen in a fortnight. That way it will give Tobias and Enna time to get to know one another," King Aegnor suggested.

"King Aegnor, with all due respect. Might I too make one request?" Tobias asked firmly. "May we return to Raveria, my older brother Adlar was due to marry his queen before the war, let him have his day before ours. Besides, you cannot assume I can get to know someone in only a fortnight, especially someone I will be spending the rest of my life with."

"Tobias, how very thoughtful of you. I see your brother is happy about this. As a thank you to your great help winning this war, I will accept your request. However, I am not a patient man and I do not like to wait. If you do not return in a fortnight the wedding is off," Aegnor said with demand in his voice. "Take my daughter with you though, it will be good for her to see what Raveria has to offer, it will be her new home," Aegnor said as he took Enna's hand and guided her to Tobias.

"It is a pleasure to meet you, Enna. Shall we go to your new homeland," Tobias said, still in awe with Enna's beauty.

"Hello Tobias, so nice to meet you. I have never been outside these city walls before, so I am eager to see what your country has to offer," she said softly.

"And do not worry about my father, he is hard to please sometimes but he would not want to miss the chance of seeing his little girl get married now would he," Enna said looking back at her father. "You do not have to throw away our allegiance if we are late, we have nothing but time for a wedding."

"Of course, not my dear. Now go, and we shall see you when you arrive," King Aegnor explained.

"Let us ride to Mouro, the capital of Raveria. We should make it there by sundown," Theo said.

The two brothers', along with Enna and Theo, left the hall and made their way back to Mouro. The remaining Raverian troops had already started making their way home. Some soldiers that still remained in Endavald guided them on their travels north. Everyone was quiet and their horses trotted back to Raveria. It was odd to everyone that there was such silence after not seeing one another for quite some time. Tobias finally broke the silence just as they crossed King's Bridge.

"Where have you two been all this time?" Tobias asked Adlar and Theo.

"It is a long story," Theo said reluctantly.

"We faced many hardships along our journey south, we were stranded on an island for a long time then got attacked by a large beast, a beast no one had seen before. When we returned home you were nowhere to be seen. Actually, hardly anyone was even in the capital. This is when we knew we had to come to aid you in battle, but of course we were late. I am glad we ended up victorious though," Adlar said in a cheery tone.

"A beast? Was it large and had spiraled horns?" Tobias asked.

"Yes, young boy," Theo said.

"That is an arivuk, they are common on islands in Fallendor," Tobias explained. "Adlar, have you been able to see anything with the crown now that you have it on? Remember why we wanted it in the first place?"

"I have not, our enemy is defeated and I have a wedding to worry about," Adlar replied.

"Well you are king and need to use it sooner or later. The crown is a valuable tool for the protection of our world, father would be disappointed if we did not utilize it properly," Tobias spoke in a kind manner to the two as Enna trotted along quietly.

"What do you mean Tobias?" Theo asked.

"When you guys departed south, I too went on

a journey," Tobias bragged. "I travelled to Rozann to seek similar help our father got when he went to the island. After we defeated the arivuk on Rozann for them, Najal, the sorcerer on the island, gave my sword the same ability to see. That is how I knew we were all in trouble," Tobias decided against telling the entire truth about his trip.

Adlar was quick to reply. "You boated all that way by yourself?"

"Of course not, I met a girl named Sabina. She was kind enough to lend a helping hand." Tobias's tone grew sad. "We became pretty close, but sadly she died in the battle," Tobias's voice saddened. Tobias's eyes watered at the very mention of Sabina's name. He had not thought of her on the journey back home. It's no wonder, the two brothers, along with Theo chatted and chatted for quite some time afterwards. Adlar and Theo could see the sadness in Tobias so were talking about anything irrelevant to their last few weeks apart. They hardly even noticed that Enna was still alongside them. Enna was either too shy or too kind to enter in any conversation, so she stayed silent. But soon, they arrived in Mouro.

Tobias cheered up at the sight of being back in Raveria. "Welcome to the capital, it is beautiful is it not?" Tobias said.

"It is rather wonderful," Enna said as she looked around at the abundance of forest and greenery.

"After my brother Adlar's wedding I can

show you around a bit," Tobias said to Enna. She replied quietly, like always. "I would like that very much."

Before the group entered the city Adlar trotted his horse in between Enna and Tobias to interrupt them as any older brother would do.

"You two will have plenty of time to talk," Adlar said. "Tobias, have you read much of father's books like I asked? Any useful knowledge to share?"

"I will be honest with you brother. I did not read a thing," Tobias stated, appearing rather embarrassed. "I remembered what Tymin told us about the island and going there was the first thing I wanted to do."

"Too busy saving the world right," Theo said sarcastically.

"Those books are meant for the king anyways, you can read them yourself, my king," Tobias rebuked with a bit of sarcasm.

"I should head back to Bedria by the way," Theo said. "My people will be worried I have not returned yet."

"Theo, you have always been the older brother I never had," Adlar explained. "I want you to stay and to be at my wedding, and stand at the front altar alongside myself and Tobias."

"I suppose I could stay a few extra days, but as soon as it is over, I will head home," Theo admitted.

"Certainly. Now if you will excuse me my

queen awaits me inside, I will read the books after the wedding, Tobias," Adlar scurried ahead of the group to be the first into the city.

"We got here quickly," Tobias said.

"Time flies when you two do not stop blabbering," Theo let off a cackle, but realized he was the only one laughing so stopped instantly. Which made Tobias and Enna smile.

"Is this where we are going to live, Tobias?" Enna asked.

"No, no we will govern a far greater city called Proda," Tobias's eyes lit up as he spoke the name.

"It is a lot nicer there. Right along the sea and just a happy place to be," Theo added.

"When will we go there then?" Enna asked again.

"We will go after the wedding," Tobias turned to Enna and placed his hand on her thigh.

"It is much better than where I have to govern," Theo frowned.

"What is wrong with the place you have to govern?" Enna asked. The three made their way inside the city.

"Nothing actually, other than the fact that some people there can be persistent and stuck in their own ways. But my castle is atop a large mountain so that is pretty brilliant I must add. I have only been there for over ten or so years, but it is actually not too bad," Theo explained.

"Come on, let's go inside," Tobias said.

Meanwhile, Livia was in the courtyard, waiting for Adlar when she heard word that Mouro troops and the king were arriving home. She ran toward Adlar when they finally made eye contact and she leaped into his arms.

"My love, it is so good to see you," Adlar said as he gave Livia a big welcoming hug.

"Myself and my maids have been keeping busy while you were gone. We have basically planned out the whole wedding. Can we get married soon? I cannot wait to be your queen. How does tomorrow sound?" Livia said in sheer excitement.

"Tomorrow sounds perfect, if it is planned already," Adlar replied with a smile.

"Oh good, it is planned. I took matter into my own hands and invited everyone the other day. I just knew we would win the war, so now we have more reason to celebrate with all of Raveria. We have invited the whole kingdom. Even the surrounding villages outside of the capital. They are all coming. Everyone in the harbor has been invited and the villages in Raveria, my father even said he would come and my cousin from Bedria has come down for it. I reckon it will be a large wedding, I always wanted a large wedding," Livia was talking so fast it appeared Adlar hadn't had an idea what she was saying.

"I am thrilled how excited you are dear. A

large wedding is what we all need; we have been through a lot and celebrations are in order," Adlar took Livia by the hand.

The two sat alone on a bench in the courtyard, that same bench upon which Tobias used to spend hours reading on or looking up in the night sky to gather his thoughts. But there was no night sky to ponder on. The stars were still an hour away from appearing. However, the evening birds were tweeting their little song they liked to sing. As if to ease the people of Mouro into the night.

"I hope those birds can sing for us at our wedding," Adlar said in appreciation of the tune's simplicity and beauty.

For the first time in a while, Livia and Adlar sat together on the bench, sharing a calm and peaceful moment. They knew life together as King and Queen would be something they would cherish for the rest of their lives. They felt like they could have sat out on the bench all night together. Adlar knew he wouldn't be able to sleep from excitement, and Livia was at ease in the presence of her dear Adlar. The King knew he shouldn't keep Livia up all night, with him being gone, she would have already had countless nights with no sleep recently. The least he could do was allow her to have a good proper sleep on the eve of their wedding day.

"Come my love, we must be heading to bed. I may read a bit to get tired myself, but you can go ahead to sleep. Tomorrow will be a magical day. I am so excited to make countless memories and share a life of happiness with you," Adlar said, as he and Livia left the courtyard and retreated to their room for the night.

CHAPTER THIRTEEN

It was a vibrant and sunny morning in the capital of the kingdom. A gorgeous day for any wedding, especially that of the kings. Fallendor was midway through the second week of the first month of summer, so the excitement was growing for all the people because of the warm temperatures.

Villagers and all who lived in Mouro had flocked into the square for the big day. Hundreds of people were already finding their spots to get a good view of the ceremony. The wedding was an hour or so away still. King Adlar looked out from atop his castle balcony to see a flood of people still entering the city. He thought to himself that if his coronation went ahead as planned then it would never have gathered this size of crowd. His crowning never happened in front of a crowd, but was quickly done in front of a small council before he accompanied Theo to Azden before the war. Adlar was without the crown for so long, and today was to be the first day he would be addressed in front of the people of Mouro with the crown on as king. The size of the crowds did not matter to Adlar, he was just overjoyed that today he got to marry the woman he had grown to love. The blue skies were as clear as ever, and that put a smile on King Adlar's face. As preparations continued, the king returned to his chambers. Livia and a couple of her house maidens were getting ready.

"Oh, sorry, I can come back," Adlar said, not wanting to interfere.
Adlar quickly grabbed one of his father's books and took it outside the door of his chamber to sit in silence. He blew off the dusty book and began to read.

3rd day of the 2nd Month of Winter of the 1198th Year

We have twins. I am so thrilled. We have two more boys in the family. Such joy for myself and Rosa. However, there seem to be complications with my dear sweet Queen. She is sick, very sick and I do not know if she will make it. The maidens think she only has a few days to live. I need my wife with me to raise these boys. The world is at peace yes, and it is a perfect time to raise a family, but I cannot bear to think of such a life without Rosa. I just hope my boys will be able to feel the happiness and joy I have had having three wonderful young boys. One day I know happiness will stay with them all forever. My eldest son brought us so much joy raising him and I hope that all of us will continue to live peacefully even if my dear Rosa passes on in this world. Starian.

Adlar finished reading, it was hard sometimes for him to read his father's books. The sadness he had knowing his father was about to lose the love of his life—and the boy's mother—hurt Adlar to read. These books were indeed meant to help Starian's sons gain knowledge from the life he had.

With every memory these books brought to Adlar, it brought back feelings of sadness or confusion because it resulted in loads of questions. A feeling he or anyone for that matter, would not want to have on their wedding day. Today was going to be a magical and happy day. Adlar stood up and figured he had read enough for one day. Livia and her maids left the room as Adlar re-entered.

"Do not look, not until later," Livia said to Adlar, not allowing him to see all the beauty that she was showing in her gown.

"My eyes are closed," Adlar smiled, as he covered his eyes and shut the door as he entered his room alone.

The wedding was approaching, and the king

was putting on his finest clothes for the ceremony. He got ready quickly, and made his way down to the courtyard where the wedding celebration would take place.

Adlar joined up with Theo and Tobias as they took their spots at the front of the courtyard. There was a very large crowd in attendance, so a stage was built for the ceremony so all could see from afar. Hundreds of people waited for the wedding to begin. The crowd seemed rowdy as local pubs had opened early to allow people to begin celebrating this momentous day in the capital. The brother's awaited signal for the wedding to begin.
"You look nervous Adlar," Theo said.
"This shirt is far too tight and it is making this heat unbearable," Adlar said tugging on his navy-blue shirt in discomfort.
"I think you wore that shirt when you were eight, it looks ridiculous," Theo replied jokingly.
"It is okay, you only have a few quick words to say and the wedding will be over. Then we can fix you with a nice cup of brandy," Tobias said calmly.
"How about four cups of brandy," Theo said with a gentle grin on his face.
"Do not joke Tobias, you're next," Adlar replied, not fazed by the joking of Theo.
"Where is Enna anyways?" Tobias asked.
"Is that not her right there in the front? In the violet dress," Theo said, pointing out to the front of

the packed crowds.

"Ah yes, beautiful she is. I am growing quite fond of her." Tobias smiled and waved at Enna.

"Alright this is taking too long. I am getting anxious. We need to begin already," Adlar said nervously.

Music played. Trumpets echoed from the city walls. The crowd turned to see Livia coming from beyond the crowds. The sight of Livia in her long silk dress and hair all done up nice made Adlar speechless like the day he first saw her in the harbor. Livia proceeded gracelessly to the front stage to join her future husband.

Livia's beauty was something else. Everyone in the crowd was in shock at her stunning look. Livia had joined the brother's and the judge, who was welcoming the people to the ceremony. Adlar couldn't stop looking at Livia.

"My word darling, you are simply beautiful. My heart races when I see your glow," Adlar whispered trying to avoid the judge hearing while he continued proceedings.

"I love you Adlar. I am so happy we are getting married; I get to be your queen," Livia whispered back.

"Quiet my dear, we cannot let the judge get us in trouble on our wedding day," Adlar, joked.

"Ladies and gentlemen, the king and queen are now going to finish this beautiful occasion by offering each other their love for one another. Please come forward to speak your vows," the judge invited Adlar and Livia to approach the front of the stage to announce their vows.

Adlar and Livia held hand and stepped forward to the front of the stage. Out of nowhere an arrow whizzed through the air piercing Livia right in the chest. Adlar was wide-eyed and silent as he reached to catch Livia from falling to the ground. A second arrow came flying in striking Theo in the stomach, followed by another arrow to his shoulder. Screams and chaos pursued as all the villagers and city folk scattered all over the streets to run for cover. Adlar rose to his feet and yelled. "Guards find whoever did this! Lock the city gate at once!"

It appeared guards already had a few men in pursuit. Hooded figures were now firing their arrows at will at the unarmed civilians. The Mouro guards disarmed some of the hooded group who were outnumbered by city soldiers. The guards slaughtered all but one. They took the hooded person to the stage to Adlar and it was revealed that it was the man that had done this. Adlar and Tobias were stunned and couldn't believe what had just happened. Livia and Theo laid on the stage breathless.

"My king, we have the scum that did this," a city guard announced who had the hostage on his knees.

Adlar was angered at the sight of the man as he rushed to him and kicked him in the face.

"Who are you? How did you get a weapon

inside? Speak!"

"You are foolish, young king. You brought me here yourself and your dead guards left a bow for me after we slit their throats," the man said, with blood running from his left eyebrow.

"I do not understand, I have the power to spare you so, tell me the truth," Adlar said back in frustration.

"You brought me here from Demar," the man said as if to mock the King. "We snuck on your ship when your men came to rescue you a moon ago. We had been laying low in the harbor waiting for our opportunity. It was so kind of your queen to invite us all to your wedding, please send her my regards," the man said as Adlar again struck him in the face with the back of his hand.

"I do love the anger you are showing. My father would be very proud of me," the hooded man said with a crooked smile.

"Your father? You mean to say that Larrius is your father?" Adlar said.

"My father, King Larrius. I reckon you know him well. My name is Manum. I am the leader of his secret group of assassins. Well, at least I was until your men slaughtered us," Manum carried on.

Adlar had a look of disgust and frustration on his reddened face. He did not wish to continue talking to Manum anymore, knowing who he was. He grabbed his guard's sword and cut off Manum's head.

"Clean up this mess," Adlar said, throwing the

bloodied sword to the ground. He then went back over to his beloved Livia and started to cry.

"Adlar, I am sorry for your loss. But we must not show weakness. Our people need us too," Tobias said, trying to console his older brother.

"Perhaps I am too weak brother," Adlar said with tears in his eyes. "My love is gone."

"I was late for the battle in Azden. I will not be able to get over this heartbreak. You are right, we cannot show weakness but I know I will not be able to bear it. You are stronger than me Tobias; you have shown it already. Father would be very proud of you; I know he had big hopes for you. You were his special boy. That is why I must abdicate the crown and hand it over to you. You are now king," Adlar said, wanting to fight back even more tears.

"Adlar, I cannot accept this. My mind is already settled in Proda," Tobias was quick to rebuke.

"It has to happen Tobias, be king of Raveria. Continue to unite the three cities of the north under your own rule. That is how father would truly want it," Adlar explained.

"I know I must be strong. Theo is also gone. We have to bring peace back to Fallendor. It has been under two months since father passed and there has already been so much death and so much violence," Tobias said, placing his arm around Adlar's shoulder.

"I can only accept this if you can promise to stay by my side, be my royal advisor or better yet, be my captain. I will need your help more than ever, be a part of this with me, I need you Adlar," Tobias said to Adlar, humbled at the offer.

"I will be by your side always," Adlar replied. "Here. I now give you the crown, King of Raveria."

"As the new king, I will demand a decree that from this day forward, the cities of Bedria, Proda and Mouro will continue to unite under only one king and a law to never go back to the ways of the past," Tobias declared.

"The cities will remain strong and cohesive with one another. I will get to the technicalities in due time. But for now, we must march to Tatilan and finish what we started," Tobias said standing by his brother's side.

Adlar and Tobias stood and spotted a small crowd of people who slowly made way back to the courtyard. A lot had happened in the last few moments, some of the people that stayed to watch the commotion had seen Adlar hand over the crown so he announced to them all.

"People of Raveria, your new king, Tobias!" Adlar shouted for all to hear. Tobias was humbled by the reception he got, he gave a smile and stepped closer to the crowd. Beside Theo and Livia, he spoke.

"My people, these are troubling times and it is my responsibility to act and to act fast. My army has already received orders to prepare for another attack. We will head to Tatilan and end their threat, once and for all. For the safety of you all I will not allow foreign invaders into our nation ever again. We will attack immediately!" Tobias said to the people.

Tobias and Adlar walked away from the people. The crowds seemed to go back to their regular lives, as they left to the markets, these last few days were not regular at all.

"This was not how I envisioned this day. The sun was shining and my wedding was a bloodbath. Our friend Theo, gone. My dear sweet…" Adlar started to cry at the very thought of Livia.

"Brother, we have to be strong. It is what father would want for us," Tobias said as the brothers walked up onto the city walls to get some space and some fresh air.

"Father knew so much, but always kept it from us. I just know that the books he left us are certainly ones where secrets will be discovered," Adlar said. "I must stay here with Livia and bury her, along with Theo."

"We have to move fast, we can say goodbye but we really should make way to Tatilan," Tobias explained. "Adlar, father knew we all wanted to be king one day. And we could not rule one nation apparently. He did what he thought would bring us all joy and happiness."

"I blame Agaras for all of this," Adlar admitted.

"As you should, that is why we must avenge everyone against him," Tobias explained calmly.

As the two brothers were perched on the city walls a small little finch flew by. Hearing the lovely melody, the bird was tweeting brought a smile to both Tobias and Adlar's face. A smile he probably didn't think would ever enter back into his life. He loved to listen to the birds whistling and singing, it gave him a sense of relief.

"Would life not be so simple if we were birds," Adlar thought out loud.

"We all have our obstacles in life. No matter how big or small. Such a peaceful little bird, making such nice noises, flying around wherever it wants. The fresh breeze and not a care in the world. In reality though that bird probably has a family and must feed its little ones for survival. It could spend all day searching for food. Someday it must come home with no food for its family at all. It would be a tiring life, but that little bird shows courage and will never give up, for the sake of its family. Even if it means risking its own life from bigger birds or other creatures. We only see things for what they appear. But in reality, every living thing has obstacles they must overcome. To that bird it could see you as someone who once was a king living a luxurious life. Peaceful and prosperous. But you too had your obstacles and you have to now, more than ever overcome them. You have the upper hand though is all I am trying to say, you have me by your side, always and forever brother," Tobias said as Adlar smiled and wiped his eyes.

The brothers looked off over the stoned walls and watched the finch fly away out of sight.

"Tobias, the way you speak, so calmly and confidently makes me know you will be a great king because you see things in so much detail, even the little things. At such a young age too, you really have started to show signs of maturity for a nineteen-year-old," Adlar said as he pat Tobias on the back.

"Come brother, we must go to your old chambers," Tobias said as they glided swiftly to the chambers.

"I have a message to send. Adlar, grab me that piece of parchment I am going to write," Tobias said frantically as they arrived at the king's room.

"A letter from your new king. King Tobias, once steward of Proda, is now the King of all Raveria. There will only be one king, like my father before me. These cities will remain united. In due time, I will re-elect Byrim as steward in Proda and a new steward in Bedria. To help me maintain order in the north. We are also on our way to attack Tatilan. They slaughtered so many innocent lives and we must show our strength to teach them a lesson. Then peace in Fallendor will be restored," Tobias spoke out loud as he wrote. "Adlar, please deliver these for guards to ride out and deliver these messages to the rest of Raveria," Tobias said, handing Adlar the parchment.

"Certainly brother," Adlar said and left the room right away.

Tobias had a thought as he sat down on his bedside and grabbed his sword. His sword allowed him to look into the mind of his enemy. Tobias also now had the crown of Raveria and it too had the same power. Tobias wondered if he used both simultaneously what power it could wield. Tobias, who had his crown on, lifted up his sword and went into the mind of his brother.

Tobias could see Agaras in his room preparing for bed, but couldn't see much else. That's it, Tobias thought to himself. Nothing had changed using both items, regardless he could still see his brother like before. Tobias would perhaps have to seek the sorcerers once more to see if they could help him utilize both the crown and the sword. There was no time to go to the island of Rozann. It was still early in the night but Tobias knew he had to rest, so he took off his crown, closed his eyes and went to sleep.

Morning had come fast and Tobias woke up from his first sleep in his new king's chamber, a relaxing sleep on a soft bed was a rare feeling to him. He was at peace when he slept, he knew though that once they set off for war his sleep would not be so peaceful at all. King Tobias was no expert of military knowledge. At such a young age and the way he felt off the glory of victory in the battle of Azden he would use that to show his confidence again. A shine entered the room of the king. The light from the sun shone through the window and gave off a huge glow from the jewel that Tobias had kept hidden. It was an amazing sight, it even surprised Tobias at the glistening light. He almost forgot he took the precious jewel from the island of Rozann. Tobias was so desperate to find out the secrets that jewel possessed, but he had other matters to attend first. He placed the jewel atop a dusty shelf, and noticed the dusty books that were left for the brothers. Tobias was realizing that his time as king would be spent reading and figuring out the secrets of this world and it's past. Adlar talked briefly of their father's writing's but didn't reveal too much. It seemed Tobias would have a lot more time on his hands than Adlar did. A wedding with Enna and a war in the south stood between Tobias and his father's mysterious writings. As the sun continued to shine through, Tobias knew the initiable war was upon him…war. Preparations for this battle had already begun as Adlar rejoined Tobias along with a few sergeants.

"The plan is simple. A large fleet of soldiers will set sail in ships across the Grey Sea to the island of Demar. Once they are there they will wait until night and get into smaller boats and sail to Tatilan. The smaller boats will not be easily seen and are much quicker when approaching the shores. I have already sent soldiers to the harbor to set sail. The rest of us will march through Azden. I have to speak to King Aegnor about postponing my wedding until my arrival back. I have already sent an early word to them to ask for their aid. The rest of us will use their smaller boats in the south and ride to the shores of Tatilan as well. When we are all stationed in Tatilan, both sets of soldier's signals to the other. I hope this signal will not be spotted by the enemy, but once the signal is made, we will attack the capital city Tapura immediately. We will attack from both the north and the east. We should both arrive in Tatilan around the same time so we must wait for a signal. We must all go now and march south to meet our Azden alleys. To war!" Tobias gave his orders as everyone prepared for battle, in hope that this would be the last battle Fallendor saw forever. It was time to move out.

CHAPTER FOURTEEN

The time had come. Raverian troops, alongside their Azden alleys, had arrived at the shores of Tatilan. The journey south had been long, but things had gone more smoothly than the last time someone tried to come this far south. Night came and went, and the morning sun rose through a foggy haze that hung over the lands of Tatilan. King Tobias and his soldiers made camp just east of Tapura, the capital city, preparing for their surprise assault.

    Tobias and Adlar did not know how making Tapura a battleground was going to benefit Fallendor. The people of Tatilan had no idea what was coming to their barren grasslands. The Treaty of Fallendor had already been broken, so the new King of Raveria was taking his chance to avenge all the lives Larrius and Agaras had taken—and to show them why they should stay within their own borders if they knew what was good for them. As his forces settled into camp, King Tobias took the opportunity to send notice to the north side of Tatilan where a second contingent of Raverian soldiers were stationed; they would need to make their own preparations for the attack to succeed. The united forces of Raveria and Azden formed a large enough army to overcome the remaining Tatilan troops—that was what King Tobias was hoping, anyway. If they could deplete the enemy's forces enough, it should keep them from retaliating and help bring about some measure of justice for all those killed in Tatilan's own attacks.

"What now?" Adlar asked Tobias, who seemed to be anxiously waiting for something.

"We must stay stationed by this mountain until the time is ready. Adlar, come with me for a moment," Tobias said, walking ahead and ducking into his tent. As his brother followed him through the tent flap, Tobias turned, sword in hand.

"I didn't want the men to see, but I think it might be wise to see what Agaras is up to this morning before we attack," Tobias said, drawing his sword and focusing his mind, channeling the blade's power as he readied himself to look into the mind of his twin brother, "If our brother has caught wind of our approach, he could well have an ambush prepared."

"Lovely morning, this," Agaras said to the lone watch guard who stood beside him upon the city walls of Tapura.

"Yes, my lord," the guard replied, sounding somewhere between anxious and exhausted.

It was apparent that Agaras was now king of Tatilan, his garb ornate and a gold crown atop his head; the guard, tired as he was, was torn between continuing and keeping his mouth shut before he irked his lord. He settled on continuing; the King seemed to be in a friendly enough mood.

"I have not seen anything on these eastern walls for weeks, sir; months, for that matter," the guard said, looking off into the distance, eyes tired and a pudgy frame slouching a bit. Agaras chuckled softly.

"You have been a true and loyal servant of your king; take the rest of the day off and tell the other guards to do so as well. Everyone deserves a bit of rest, and I doubt there will be any sudden crises after all this time," King Agaras said to the overjoyed guard.

"Thank you, my King!" The guard beamed and jogged off; his prior lethargy forgotten in the face of unexpected leisure time.

Agaras looked down from the city walls with a smile on his face. He was at peace for the first time in…well, in his whole life, really. He felt real happiness knowing that he was finally King, no matter what it had cost him to get there; this was where he belonged, crowned and powerful. Agaras had felt trapped under Larrius' control, but standing here on his walls, gazing out across his city, at the heart of his kingdom, here, in this moment, for maybe the only time he could think of, Agaras truly felt important.

"Adlar, you will not believe what I just saw." Tobias huffed, sheathing his sword as the vision faded.

"What was it?" Adlar asked, with worry on his face.

"Our brother Agaras is now King of Tatilan—and he just gave his watch guards the day off! Now is the perfect time to attack!" Tobias said with a grin on his face.

"Should I send word for the troops to mobilize?" Adlar questioned, his own countenance sliding into its own smile.

"Yes, brother, prepare for the attack. Send a messenger to signal the men stationed to the north to attack as well," Tobias said. "Then pick a few men to make for the city walls—ones who know how to move without drawing too much attention. They shouldn't be seen while all the guards are taking their little break; the chance to scale the walls and rappel down the other side is too good to miss. If they do it quickly and quietly, they can unlock the gate for us, and we can push right on in without any sort of extended battle."

"The timing will have to be perfect," Adlar said, "I'll send our best infiltrators ahead."

Tobias nodded in acknowledgment, and Adlar saluted and strode from the tent. A few moments later, Tobias took a deep breath and rose from his seat, grabbing his helmet and marching out to address his troops.

"Men, prepare for battle!" Tobias shouted to his assembled soldiers.

The Raverian men were already geared up in their shining armor, clearly fired up and ready for a fight. A cheer rose from their milling ranks as they hastened into formation at their king's words. As they finished forming up, Tobias moved to the head of their column.

"We will station ourselves a little closer to the city walls, just below the tip of the hill. When we see the gate open, we charge!" Tobias yelled for all the soldiers to hear, and squad officers relayed his orders back through the rear echelons where not even his powerful voice could reliably carry. With a great clanking of armor and tromping of boots and hooves, the army moved out.

Long minutes later, the joint Raverian and Azden forces fidgeted in the shadow of the hill and waited for the gate to open. Adlar had sent his hand-picked men ahead to scale the walls and open the gate some time ago, and yet, after several excruciating minutes of waiting, no gate had opened, and the King was beginning to worry. If the infiltrators had been caught….

"Adlar, did you not send your men in?" Tobias asked, though he was sure he knew the answer; his brother was a perfectly competent commander, and he could hardly have forgotten such an important task.

"Yes; a full squad of our best, quietest men. They should already be in by now," Adlar replied, his own frustration and concern clear in the furrow of his brows and the tension in his voice.

The army waited on for what felt like an eternity. Men started to get restless, especially the Azden soldiers, heavily armed and on horseback. They would be the first ones to charge the city, the tip of the spear. Their ranks formed the army's front line, and they were clearly impatient to charge forward. Tobias was beginning to worry that his allies might decide that a foreign king's orders were less interesting than the glory of battle. Then, finally, the gates opened. Tobias' eyes lit up as he yelled for the cavalry to attack.

"Charge!"

The cavalry launched themselves forward before the word had even fully left his lips, followed by the infantry, pounding forward more slowly but with just as much eagerness. The sound of the approaching forces could've been heard from miles away as they stormed across the dusty Tatilan plains.

The hundreds of racing horsemen reached the

city well ahead of the rest of the Raverian and Azden soldiers, weapons raised and hooves thundering—and the city gates slammed down, sealing the walls anew. Throngs of archers appeared all along the walls, and a dark cloud of arrows rose up into the morning sky, casting a shadow across the land.

"Shields!" Adlar yelled, waving his men into what cover there was as he braced his own shield overhead and hoped that it would be enough. Adlar's shield held, but there were simply too many arrows and the cavalry were too flatfooted to react; dozens of men and horses fell, a large portion of the cavalry decimated on the spot.

The rest of the army continued their run for the gate; they were committed now, but their earlier enthusiasm had drained away in favor of grim determination. If they couldn't breach those walls one way or another, their losses in a retreat would be catastrophic, the archers simply tearing them apart from the safety of the walls. Thankfully for Tobias' forces, it seemed that the city's defenders were not organized enough for a similarly devastating second volley, and the majority of the remaining soldiers made it to the wall for cover, though not without taking heavy losses to the more sporadic waves of arrows that followed the first.

"What do we do now?" Adlar yelled, taking cover from the archers on the wall above him. They needed a way in, fast; bows might not be easy to aim at this range, but there was little to stop the defenders from simply dropping heavy stones on the heads of any attacker not directly under a crenellation.

"They cannot get us from up there when we stand this close to the walls—not with their bows, anyway, and we have our own archers if they decide to lean out too far. We just have to continue to wait," Tobias shouted in reply as he huddled up closer to the wall. "And hope your men are good enough to get those damn doors open!"

As they waited, men being picked off slowly but steadily, a large group of soldiers piled into the arch of the gate, sheltering within its frame for better cover and hacking at the huge, iron-barred oak doors with axes and hatchets; unfortunately, Tobias could see that they were making only slow progress, and he doubted they'd be able to tell the gate in time to do anyone any good. He grimaced. This was going poorly. The angle of the top of the walls didn't allow for the archers to get a good view of the men under them, so, for now, the Raverian and Azden soldiers were mostly safe, but huddling against the enemies' walls and hoping to chop the great gates down with hand axes before his men starved or tried to run and became pincushions wasn't a great position to be in. Then, suddenly, a commotion could be heard from inside the city—screams, shouts, the sounds of swords clashing and armor clanging. Then there was a moment of silence before, without further warning, the gate opened with a lurch. To the amazement of the startled troops at the gate, axes still raised, they found themselves facing a squad of battered, bloodied Raverian troops. It was the soldiers from the northern detachment, finally making their way into the city to aid the others, but they had clearly suffered huge losses on the way, and the soldiers' relief at friendly faces was short-lived as a cloud of arrows buzzed down from the walls, hammering into the exhausted Raverian's, dropping them nearly to a man. The gate was open, though, and that was what Tobias needed.

"Soldiers, attack!" Tobias yelled to his men as they swarmed in through the gate and over the fallen soldiers that had already been laid to waste by the Tatilan army inside. Dead horses and bloodied men littered the streets as Tapura became a bloody communal grave for the dead of both armies.

"Take down those archers!" Adlar yelled as the Tatilan bowmen continued to fire freely into his forces. Azden archers fired back at the men on the walls, and without the benefit of crenellations and a mob of furious soldiers pouring up the ramparts, it wasn't long before the threat of archers on the wall had been dealt with.

The fight continued throughout the city, and King Agaras finally emerged to join the battle as the front pushed closer and closer to the city center. Agaras was an exceptional swordsman and it showed, his blade flashing in the sun as he carved a path through his former people with ease. One by one, Agaras slew his opposition as he fought his way across the castle courtyard, drenched in the blood of those he had killed, his own armor barely scratched by the men in his way. Still, he was just one man, and the Tatilan numbers were dropping quickly. Tapura was being overrun, and as King Agaras laid eyes on his brother Adlar, he snarled and changed directions, storming toward his sibling with murder in his eyes.

"Are you going to fight me, brother?" Agaras yelled, hate contorting his face.
"It is over, brother, you cannot defeat us now. You are outnumbered, and you alone cannot defeat an entire army!" Adlar yelled back, and the battle seemed to come to a standstill around the two.

Tobias saw the confrontation from a distance, and swore, fighting his way through the milling throngs to reach his brothers.

"Surrender now, Agaras, and we can spare your life, and so many other innocent lives. We can have peace once more," Tobias yelled across the bloodied courtyard, struggling to be heard over the melee that continued to swirl around Agaras and Adlar.

"I am sorry, brothers," Agaras replied calmly, and lowered his sword. Adlar's eyes widened in surprise and, for a split second, he began to smile, when Agaras' other hand suddenly lashed out. There was a soft whistling and a meaty *thunk*, and Adlar grabbed at his throat, gurgling around the blade of the throwing knife lodged there. Blood poured from his mouth and he fell to his knees. Adlar tried to speak, but he was choking on his own blood too much to form the words, and within an instant he had collapsed to the ground.

"No!" Tobias cried out, sprinting furiously toward Agaras as he finally broke free of the crowd. Agaras turned, surprised by his twin's speed, and barely managed to dodge as Tobias swung his sword, fast as a viper. That was just the first blow, though, and Agaras instantly found himself on the defensive, struggling to dodge or parry a hail of frenzied strikes. Soon, though, Agaras wasn't fast enough; Tobias knocked aside Agaras' own desperate strike, then, fast as lighting, turned his swing into a backstroke. Agaras howled as the tip of his brother's blade scored a blazing line of pain across his face, staggering back then toppling to the ground, clutching his face in both hands as he stumbled over the bodies of his and his brothers' men. Agaras rolled on the ground in agony as he screamed, eventually rising, gasping, to his knees. When his hands came away from his face, this time they were red with his own blood—though he would never see that, as Tobias' sword had slashed across both his eyes, leaving a grisly red seam across his features, a curtain of red pouring down across his cheeks. Agaras panted and gasped, barely suppressing his pain, and turned his head to face Tobias with his bloodied eyes, and it was clear that even if he couldn't see he still knew death was upon him.

"Go on, do it!" Agaras said.

"You do not deserve to live! You killed father, you killed Tymin, and you killed Adlar! You are the reason so many innocent people lost their lives. You do not deserve to live," Tobias said as he raised his sword. The rest of the soldiers on both sides had stopped fighting; it was clear who was the victor here. Agaras moaned miserably.

"I never killed father. It was Maria," Agaras admitted, "It was her idea. She poisoned him. I told her once that the only way I could ever be King of Raveria was if I convinced him to declare me heir over the rest of you. Maria said she knew someone who could get us a brew, something with a kind of magical source in it that would compel whoever drank it to obey, at least for a certain length of time." Agaras grimaced.

"Maria went to a nearby village and came back with the brew," he continued. "We suspect that she told the man too much of her plan, and he gave her the wrong potion on purpose. She snuck the poison into his wine one night, not understanding what it really was, and not long after he got sick, and not long after that, he died. When I tried to convince father to name me his heir, before the sickness fully took hold, it became clear that the brew was not working as I had expected. Father seemed to know what was happening, so I ran off and told Maria that if word got out, I would take the blame for whatever happened to protect her. A day or two later, he died," Agaras was in tears by this point, watery tracks blending with the blood that still dripped down his face. Tobias was appalled by what Agaras had just told him.

"If you would have just been honest from the beginning then we would all still be alive!" Tobias shouted, outraged, "Why did you lie, Agaras? When you told me by the lake that you killed father, I was devastated! I could have helped you if you'd just told me from the beginning that it was Maria!"

"I was scared! I had been hearing voices in my head for weeks before that, things were falling apart—I didn't want to get in trouble, I didn't want Maria to be blamed! I loved her so much," Agaras said, his voice dejected and hoarse.

"You are a fool, brother," Tobias said, disgusted.

"Well, then just kill me! Do it, you coward!" Agaras yelled back, wiping the blood from his face. Tobias paused, taken aback for a moment. Then he sighed.

"I am sorry brother; perhaps the better thing would be to spare your life and leave you to suffer in your blindness," Tobias said, speaking more calmly now as he wiped his sword clean and sheathed it.

"Goodbye, brother," Tobias said over his shoulder, turning away from the carnage and death, "I doubt the pain of that wound will ever leave you; you certainly will not see again." Tobias turned to his men as the defeated Tatilan forces yielded with little fuss. They knew a loss when they saw one, and this one had been…decisive.

"Men, let's go. Leave the dead, but bring back

my brother Adlar's body," Tobias said, walking toward the gate. The people of Tapura were slowly creeping out of their homes to see what was happening in the courtyard and find out why the commotion had stopped. Tobias noticed them and gave them one final message.

"People of Tatilan! Never again will your people come north to Azden or Raveria. We wish only to remain at peace, that we can all live independently and prosperously, but we will not hesitate if the time should come that war is needed. Your people struck at ours, broke your treaties, killed our citizens. We have repaid that debt. No more violence shall come to Fallendor for as long as I am King of Raveria, unless you and yours decide to provoke it. Now, your King, Agaras, is blind and needs your help. I leave it to you to decide what that means," Tobias said, leading his forces, somber and battered but victorious, from the city of Tapura, taking one last look of despair at his brother, "Farewell, my brother. I have a wedding to go home to, but I wish things could have ended differently between us."

CHAPTER FIFTEEN

It was the wedding day of King Tobias and Enna. The war of Tatilan was over, and peace had been restored. In Tobias' mind, everyone had lost because this was a battle that he would dwell on for quite some time. Yet, still there was time for a joyous occasion. Raverian forces had settled in and returned home in the North. The wedding of King Tobias and Enna was scheduled for that afternoon in the city of Mouro and folks from all over Fallendor were expected to attend. Even people from Azden made their way north for the first time in their lives. It was to be a very momentous day indeed for this was the very first time a man and woman would marry from opposite sides of the border, one from Azden and one Raveria. This special occasion would surely signify an everlasting bond between the two great nations.

Tobias was lost in a sea of racing thoughts. He has secrets to share and had to speak with Enna urgently.

"I must tell you something," Tobias said. Enna stretched her arms as she yawned and stepped out of bed. "What is it?" she asked.

"I have so much to tell you, and in time you will know everything. Right now, I must reveal to you the power of my sword. It gives me the rare ability to see into the mind of my enemy, my brother Agaras. Since we are now at peace; I want to bury the sword and its information and confess that this is how I was able to help us win the war. I want to get rid of it, and avoid any further corruption it may lead to. I felt compelled to tell you about this power," Tobias said, pulling out his sword.

"I think you should keep it. Perhaps it may be useful to you again someday. Why not hide it for safekeeping just in case?" Enna answered.

"The crown lost its power, since it died with Adlar, but the power of this sword remains," Tobias replied.

"Can you use it and show me how it works," Enna suggested.

"I will show you how it works," Tobias said. "Stand back my love." Tobias lifted the sword and entered into the mind of his brother one last time.

Enna was bewildered at the sight of Tobias

who stood there with closed eyes, as beads of sweat fell from his brow. King Tobias opened his eyes and looked as shocked as Enna.

"What is it?" Enna asked.

"I am confused. I cannot say anything right now, but I promise to tell you after the wedding," Tobias said. "Ah, there is so much I must confess, but it is time to prepare for our wedding."

"Keep the sword here, until we need it again. Everything will be okay, let's get ready," Enna said, grabbing Tobias arm with a kiss.

The ceremony commenced. Hundreds, perhaps thousands of people packed inside the city to witness history. Tobias was alone at the front stage, the very same stage that his brother Adlar and Livia stood upon many weeks ago. Tobias was confident the same fate would not follow him. Although Byrim was there with Tobias, he felt alone, he realized standing up in front of all, that his brother Adlar was not here with him on such a big day. The blue skies were very reminiscent of that fateful day during the last wedding that occurred in Mouro. It seemed to always be a beautiful day when a wedding was to occur in the capital. Tobias rose his head up to the clear blue skies and breathed a deep breath of fresh air as he relaxed himself. A bird fluttered by tweeting a joyful sound making Tobias smile.

The sound was overpowered by the noise of horns and instruments. Enna was coming down a path to begin the wedding. Her shining hair was hanging low and her silk dress shined from the beaming sunlight. Her smile was from ear to ear and could be seen from the stage where Tobias awaited her. Tobias was quickly joined by Enna and he couldn't stop smiling as he greeted her on stage.

"My word Enna, you look beautiful," Tobias said as he grabbed her by the hand.

"You are kind, but many thanks to my handsome king," Enna replied with a charming smile.

The city judge stood between the two and began proceedings.

"Welcome all, we are gathered here for the united bond of King Tobias and his Queen, Enna. Through marriage Raveria will be fully allied with Azden. Welcome all travelers that join us here today. The ale and wine will be flowing out tonight in celebration. First, we ask these two to announce their love for one another and bring forth the rings," the judge said.

"Tobias, I have known you for a very short while but, since then I have always felt your love. The strength and devotion you show is endless. I love you, take this ring as a symbol of my love for you," Enna said, placing the ring on Tobias' finger.

"Enna, my dear sweet Enna. I met you at a difficult time in my life. I have been faced with many hardships at such a young age. Even since I've known you, I have been through a lot. You have shown me nothing but love and for that I thank you. You are so patient, strong and loving to me always. Take this ring as a symbol of my love for you. And also, take this crown, my Queen. I welcome you now to Raveria as my wife, and as Queen of Raveria," Tobias said, placing the crown upon Enna's head, and the ring on her finger.

"You may now kiss, to show your love for one another," the judge said. The two kissed, it felt like the weight of so many lives had been lifted for Tobias.

"King and Queen of Raveria!" the judge yelled to a loud cheer from the crowds.
Tobias and Enna kissed again and celebrations proceeded quickly. The king and queen stepped through the crowds to cheers and joy. The wedding was as beautiful as Enna's blue eyes. Tobias smiled so big that he began to laugh.

Market vendors rolled out barrels of ale and people were quick to grab a drink. There were tables of food and loads of beverages as joy had finally come to this wonderful city.

Through the chaos, Tobias met eyes with Maria. His mind was racing with confusion, did he trust what his brother said or was she innocent, Agaras had lied to him before, so he thought it could happen again.

"Maria, I am surprised to see you here," Tobias said. Enna holding onto his strong forearm, wondering herself who this woman could be.

"I have been here my whole life, why leave

now?" Maria asked. Her skin flourished its natural color and her hair was combed and tied up tightly, a rare look for her.

"Agaras told me that you killed my Father. I will have you hung for this, what say you?" Tobias asked, with uncertainty.

"Agaras is alive?" Maria's eyes lit up. She smiled, but returned her lips shut quickly.

"I don't understand what you are talking about, I could never do such a thing," Maria said.

Tobias clenched his jaw. He never liked being lied to, and now he was stuck in two thoughts, believe Agaras who framed Maria or believe Maria, who never truly made sense anyway.

"This is not the time for a discussion, if this was not my wedding day, I would see you in irons, but for now we will pause such quarrels."

Enna popped out in between the two.

"Tobias, let's go, it is our wedding day, we will deal with her later," Enna said. The blue of her eyes lured Tobias in. They shared a grin.

"Maria, your fate will be dealt with soon, excuse us."

Tobias and Enna rejoined the party.

"I have a bad feeling about her," Enna said. The crowds were loud from celebrations. Tobias's brow rose.

"Quite the party my dear, don't worry about Maria, she will be dealt with accordingly," Tobias said. He couldn't stop smiling at his beautiful new queen, but she didn't return the same look.

"You should have arrested her, despite being our wedding day."

"Oh, come on Enna, we don't want any trouble on our special day, if she's telling the truth there's no reason to worry, there's Byrim, let's go see him."

Byrim came bundling in. You could pick him off from a mile away, he was certainly one of the tallest in the whole crowd. Byrim laughed when he laid eyes on Tobias, a large pint of ale in both hands, spilling onto the dresses of locals dancing.

"Tobias, this is for you," Tobias accepted the glass, knowing full well Byrim had enough already.

"Thanks, cousin. We have to get going though, so many faces to see and people to talk to. We will catch up later."

Enna rushed ahead to her father and mother and gave them a large hug. Tobias noticed them laughing and smiling while he got lost in his own thoughts again. He was distracted by the yelling and screaming of the celebratory crowds. Staring at Enna's beauty, Tobias smiled. She looked back to wave him over. Her pupils grew when she noticed the puzzled look on his face so she walked back toward Tobias. Tobias shook his head to wake himself up and approached Enna promptly, before joining her parents, Aegnor and Elena.

"What is it Tobias?" Enna asked.

"It's just what I saw when I was in my

brother's mind, I can't stop thinking about it," Tobias said.

"And?"

"I saw Agaras, he was not alone," Tobias said quietly. "He was with a familiar face, he was with Najal, the sorcerer from Rozann. I don't know how he even got there. It looked like he gave Agaras something."

"What was it? Who is Najal? Why is this bad?" Enna said, seemingly worried now. Her voice grew louder, but didn't want anyone to over hear, if that was even possible with the cheering happening.

"Najal gave me the ability to see into my enemies mind. We spoke and he talked about a source of power they could harness if they could get to the other side of the island. I helped them be able to do such a thing," Tobias said anxiously.

"Najal seemed angry when he was with my brother Agaras," Tobias continued looking straight into Enna's eyes.

"Well did Najal say anything?" Enna asked again.

Tobias paused for a moment and looked off into the crowds of people.

"Yes, Najal spoke. He said, 'This is perfect, but now we must wait eighteen years until we can rule Fallendor together, we must get back that jewel…"

Enna had a similar look as Tobias, but Aegnor and Elena had grown impatient and wanted to welcome their boy to the family.

"I'll explain everything to you later," Tobias whispered.

"Welcome, to the family young boy," King Aegnor said, squeezing the breath out of Tobias with a large hug.

"Come, on let's get a drink, we have celebrations to enjoy," Tobias said excitedly.

The look he gave Enna made her feel like Tobias had something much bigger to tell her, but it would have to wait until the crowds of Mouro dispersed and they had some privacy, whenever that would be. A joyous and happy occasion had come at a great time for all of Raveria. People were dancing and laughing and having a perfectly wonderful time. For now peace was restored in the world of Fallendor.

Tobias took Enna's soft hand and they pushed through the crowds and danced on their wedding day until the sun went down.

About the Author

Noah Cavalier is an author from a small town in Ontario, Canada called Perth. Fallendor The Sword of Sight, is his first published book in what he hopes to be the kickstart to many more books in the Fallendor series.

Noah didn't always enjoy writing, but his love for adventure and fantasy fiction was there even as he got older. After getting into reading more at an older age he began to think to himself, *hmm it would be so amazing to be able to create your own world like these great authors did,* and that is where Noah started to think, why can't I do this? It was as simple as purchasing a notebook with lined paper and stocking up on fancy pencils. The first few months gained traction and Noah went through many pencils just creating the world of Fallendor. Then it all went away, that drive disappeared. Flash forward almost three years and Noah's black book had collected its share of dust. Noah was inspired and motivated to finish his book, which at the time only had one complete chapter done. He finally made time to write and get the book you hold today finished.

Noah still spends most of his days working as a personal trainer, but when he isn't busy working or going out on his own adventures, he is plotting his second book, which hopefully won't take as long as the first book took to get finished.

Manufactured by Amazon.ca
Bolton, ON

14481492R00120